No time to stand around brooding, he told himself. He had to get this prize of his off Grady's Ground, and not later than tonight. It should be in a proper government lab. All the alie̶ ̶ ̶ ̶ ̶ ̶ ̶ ̶ ̶ ̶ ̶ ̶ ̶ ̶ ̶ ̶ ̶ ̶ ̶o a proper lab!

He needed a ̶ ̶ ̶ ̶ ̶ ̶ ̶ ̶ ̶ ̶ ̶ ̶ ̶ ̶ ̶ ̶ ̶ ̶ ̶ff into?

On the verge ̶ ̶ ̶ ̶ ̶ ̶ ̶ ̶ ̶ ̶ ̶ ̶ ̶ ̶ ̶ ̶ ̶ ̶ h for suitable containers ̶ ̶ ̶ ̶ ̶ ̶ ̶ ̶ ̶ ̶ ̶ ̶ ̶ ̶ ̶ ̶ ̶ ̶ around— he checked, sta ̶ ̶ ̶ ̶ ̶ ̶ ̶ ̶ ̶ ̶ ̶ ̶ ̶ ̶ ̶g to the . . . device?

He stared. Yes! From the small glowing ovoid, the pattern of light was now *oozing*—permeating the bowl-like base, spreading into the larger ovoid, infecting the three objects piled above!

"Oh my God!" Bennett whispered.

For the process was not stopping when it reached the limits of the alien substance. It was spreading still further —staining the very air with radiance and taking on the shape of something as incomprehensible, as majestic and as fearful as the place from which its scattered parts had come. He gasped . . . and the inhalation drew with it some of the stained and colored air.

There was a sensation like a blow delivered to—not his physical brain, but—his abstract mind, and he collapsed on the floor without another sound.

AGE OF MIRACLES

by John Brunner

ace books
A Division of Charter Communications Inc.
1120 Avenue of the Americas
New York, N.Y. 10036

Like needles thrust into a wax doll, images stabbed him.

During the summer there was plenty to eat. The fox avoided the place where his world was being invaded: the clanking mysteries, the smoky smells, the bellowing bipeds. Summer ended. For a while there was mud. Rain soaked his coat and sharpened the edge of the wind. By frost there was a hard place and a succession of stinking roars and flashes. The fox turned aside, slinking back into the long grass and the bushes. The grass became dry and yellow, the bushes stood out bare as an engraving against the sky.

Snow brought scarcity.

The fox grew resigned to the new thing in his world. It was not a change he understood, but neither could he control it. Printing his traces in the snow, breaking through the thin frozen crust although lack of food was lightening him daily, he came to the borderline and paused—not for reflection, but because a complex balance of instinctual drives was seesawing between *hunger here* and *unknown there.*

A roar began. Automatically the fox ran forward. It was his last action but one.

Afterwards, when they had cleared away the wreckage and the bodies—including the fox's—men came with guns and searched the area. His vixen and his last litter of cubs were shot. On the new road cars went cautiously as winter spread the concrete with a glaze of ice.

He moaned in darkness. Wet, clammy, unpleasant, something slimy on his face, his chest, the front of his legs. Lying in the dirt he battled ghosts.

The man—something familiar about him—in a place lit by candles, windowless, the door locked and barred against intruders . . . working. But pausing every few seconds to look around him nervously.

We know very little about them. A sardonic curl of the lip, here. We know beyond a doubt that they can set off fissionables at an indefinite distance because we learned that the hard way.

(No, it wasn't funny.)

Another nervous glance, and back to work. Knowledge is the first weapon. People generally say we're fighting in the dark, but you can't call it fighting when you don't know what your enemy is or even whether he regards you as his (?) enemy. We must find that out!

(Was that a noise? A footfall? Nothing to be seen . . . of course.)

After a petrified pause, the conclusion that it was a trick of overactive imagination. Something found now, something to claim all attention and generate pulse-pounding excitement. Could it possibly . . . ?

He lay alone in the darkness, soaked with thin wet mud, and writhed as violently as if the blow had been physical in this instant of time.

Blasphemy! The howl came, the blow followed, then the laughs of triumph. (Shalt not suffer a witch to live.)

Seek to probe the secrets of what is hidden not in knowledge but in faith! Blasphemer!

Spittle on his face. Like maddened animals all around. A snag-toothed mouth grown to enormous size, stretching from horizon to horizon and speaking the dogmas. If you would enter the holy city among the shining angels go in humility not arrogance, blasphemer and upstart!

After that, boots: kicking again and again.

He tried to crawl away, and his eyes opened. For a little he could not see and thought he must be blind. Then he rolled over, the mud plopping; its sour taste was in his mouth. Man the crown of creation (irony) lying in dirt like a hog in its wallow.

Anger burst out and bloomed in him like a fireball, lighting the landscape of his mind with a beautiful and deadly brilliance. Who put him here in the dirt? Who threw him down in a ditch like a dead dog?
He did.

The man began to pick himself up, clawing at the sides of the trench for a purchase. He felt the horrible clay fill the space between his nails and his fingertips, foul as feces. His limbs were like wooden rods, uncontrollable. He was about three-quarters dead, but his mind was alive with hate.

Dark—night—dark—night . . .

Over the lip of the ditch he saw lights and thought of lights he had seen before. He desired to go towards them. Clawing, scrabbling, thrusting, he tried to force himself up and out. Failed, and fell back. Like a man handcuffed in a cell awaiting the torturers' return, he railed against the slippery clay, his weak body, his powerlessness. White-hot, the hate crumbled his humanity as lava can crumble a peasant's hut on the slopes of Etna.

Inhuman, he found neither time nor space so impassable a barrier as the sides of this deep trench.

When the figure appeared in the restaurant, everything stopped. Only for one moment was a man's high-pitched voice raised into the appalling silence, closing a bargain with a woman for the night. And then nothing. The remembered sound of chattering and music hung in the air like dust.

His mere presence was a slap in the face. To look at him was to realize what he was, and recall that all humanity had been disgustingly insulted. Not the mask of the Red Death, not Naaman white with leprosy, could have chilled the company as this man did.

Ripped, his clothes hung from him like the bannering rags on a scarecrow made of poles. Dirty brown mud glistened wet on his face, chest and legs. He left smeared footprints as he lurched across the restaurant's floor.

Seconds passed. There were a few half-hearted screams, but it was clear from the focused intensity of the man's burning glare, from the straight-line course he was following, that he was concentrated on one individual among those present. For what? Vengeance? You could not be sure. In this Age of Miracles, you could not be sure of anything.

He's after someone, Den Radcliffe thought. It seemed a vaguely silly idea, like the delusive insights of a dream full of surreal absurdities. *Me. He's coming directly towards me.*

The tick-tock of heartbeats told him that time was passing; so did the foot-dragging approach of the stranger. Nothing else did. As though sunk in a block of transparent plastic he sat rigid beside his companions at the table. The width of the table, at least, was between himself and the intruder.

The distance narrowed to twelve paces, ten, eight. Suddenly the girl on his left—he knew her only as Maura—screamed and leaped to her feet, and others imitated her. The spell broke. Den Radcliffe could move, do something to drive away this horror, break it, smash it, this obscenity walking like a man!

He snatched up what his hand encountered on the table: a heavy glass pitcher full of water. He hurled it, and it struck the man's shoulder, making him check his stride for a second while its contents slopped some of the mud from his cheek.

A bottle, caught around the neck for a club. On his feet now, Den Radcliffe felt all his nerves sing back to life, stinging as a limb stings when circulation returns after tourniquet-like cramp. Bottle raised, liquor spouting from its neck and flowing down his sleeve, he waited in the vain hope of help.

The man spoke. His nauseous screeching voice filled the room like air rushing into a punctured vacuum. "Damn you!" he howled. "Damn you damn you *damn* you! You did this to me, you bastard!"

Superstition, against his will, shattered the self-control which Radcliffe had already weakened with drink. He swung the bottle and let it go. It broke on the man's forehead, gashing the skin, scattering with a tinkle across the floor, and then there was the long-repressed panic.

Chairs crashed over, tableclothes were dragged unheeded by scrambling fighting crazy-milling men and women, shedding cutlery and plates ringing and breaking. The waiters went with the rest; so did the musicians from the band, using their instruments as clubs, and a hundred people were rushing the yard-wide exit door before the manager turned on the ceiling panic sprays and oblivion came sifting down like snow.

Still the ghastly figure stood facing Radcliffe. He hurled

11

things at it like wooden balls at a cockshy—bottles, glasses, what his hands chanced on. The tableknifes would not throw; their handles were too heavy. A plate caught the air and swung aside, like a badly aimed discus.

He heard the hissing of the panic sprays, and terror seized him. For all he knew, the *other* confronting him might not breathe, might now draw in air and be immobilized by the anesthetic. He snatched his own last lungful before the gas came down, hooked his hands under the table's edge and lifted it with insane violence from the floor. As it came up, he somehow got another purchase on its underside so that he leaned forward into it and turned it, brought it slamming down on the impassive, hate-auraed figure, and fell forward, triumph coloring his slide into unconsciousness. After him tumbled and clattered his past and his hopes for the future.

II

"The history of the last years of the twentieth century," Waldron said under his breath, "is going to be the story of how nothing happened."

"What was that?" Across the desk Canfield—suspicious, touchy—stiffened, sure he was being snidely insulted.

"Nothing," Waldron said. "Go on."

That is, he added without even moving his lips, *if anyone bothers to write history again.*

Canfield was still glaring at him, his dark face full of hostility. Abruptly unable to bear that scowl any longer, Waldron snapped, "Go on, damn it! You came to give a report, so spit it out."

Canfield grunted and turned back the leaves of his notebook. He said, "I took a crew down to the City of Angels as soon as the call came. It was a shambles, but the manager had turned on the panic sprays. According to him, the weirdo just appeared, on the dais inside the entrance by the hat-check booth, and walked straight across the room towards one particular table. He watched it happening from a sealed armor-glass compartment on the—"

"I know the City of Angels," interrupted Waldron. And, as he saw self-righteous disapproval gather in Canfield's mind, added, "I go there all the time! When I can afford to, anyhow."

He made no attempt to interpret Canfield's reaction in words, but the latter pursed his lips hard for several seconds, as though forcibly blocking off a sharp retort, before he continued.

"Of course, it's ridiculous to say that the weirdo just *appeared*. I brought in the doorman and the bouncer, naturally, and questioned them on the way—they missed most of the gas because they were right next to the exit. Either they're lying or they panicked and don't want to admit it."

Leaning back in his chair and closing his eyes, Waldron said, "What state was this weirdo in when you picked him out from under the table?"

His train of thought broken, Canfield hesitated. "Filthy," he said at last. "Smeared with wet mud, ragged, bruised—but some of that was due to things being thrown at him, I guess."

"A man in that state wouldn't be let into the City of Angels through the main entrance," Waldron said. "I'm not asking you to speculate. Just tell me what you found when you arrived."

Canfield shut his notebook and rose to his feet, his mouth working, his Adam's apple bobbing on his stringy neck. He said, "What the hell are you trying to do—make me angry enough to give you an excuse for throwing me off the force?"

"Shut up and sit down," Waldron said. "Or if you don't want to go on, give me your notebook and I'll pick the details out of it myself."

Canfield took another few heartbeats to boil over. Then he threw the notebook on the desk in front of his chief—it made a noise like an open-handed slap—and strode out, slamming the door. The ill-fitting windows rattled in their frames; the pencils on the desk rattled against each other.

It seemed suddenly very dark in the room, although the high swinging lightbulb was new and free of dust. Waldron sat a while without moving, looking at the black cover of the notebook.

The story of how nothing happened . . .

That was what was going to break James Arnott Waldron: the hysterical pretense that it was still the same old world. One day he was going to scream at some idiot like Canfield and say, "How the hell dare you claim that you are Man, the lord of creation? You're a rat, you're an insect, you're a dirty little crawling louse scavenging after the angels—a dung-beetle butting at your ball of muck and fooling yourself that you're trundling the sun!"

Why do I hang on here? What's the point? Why don't I simply quit?

His eyes drifted from the oblong of the notebook to the oblong of a map on the wall—not the city map, the hemisphere map. That bore handmade additions and amendments; you couldn't buy a commercial or even a government-issue map which showed the world as it really was. Consequently he was not altogether certain his was accurate. But it was as truthful as he could make it. Not from masochism, as Canfield and so many other of his colleagues seemed to think. From honesty.

Why can't they understand it's necessary?

The pockmark gaps in the neat mesh of human symbols —the devastated areas, the fallout zones, into which the lines of highways and railroads led like footsteps over precipices—*had* to be included on the printed map; it would be beyond anybody's powers of self-deception pretend that Omaha, for instance, still existed. (Though of course you didn't have to keep stating aloud that the city had gone.) But the heavy black border isolating a tongue-shaped area in the center of North America, the other similar border surrounding a kidney-shaped zone in Western Brazil, and the patches of silver foil like distorted pentagroms which indicated the alien cities—those, Waldron had applied himself the day after he grew tired of the popular fiction that governments in Washington and Ottawa still held sway over the whole of their former territories.

"One day," Waldron declared to the uncaring air, "I'll wire up a bell and some flashing lights and stick a sign under the map saying DON'T KID YOURSELF. And fix it so it comes on when the door is opened."

But he knew he wouldn't go that far. It was all very well to insist that people must face the facts; it would take more than words, whether written or spoken, to bring the result about.

He was as scared as anybody else. He was as ready to hide from reality as anybody else. All he had as margin was a kind of shame. He could easily lose it. Maintaining its original force was straining his nerves. Otherwise he wouldn't have snapped at Canfield.

He drove himself to pick up the notebook at last and flip through its pages, seeing the familiar shorthand it was filled with, as clear and as easy to read once you had the context as ordinary print.

Is that symptomatic? So many of us now seem to need to do small things perfectly, as though we're resigned to giving up the big things . . . for good and all.

He hoped not. He thought of his own laborious attempts to perfect Beethoven's Opus III, first without a wrong note or shaky time-value, then without a flaw of expression. He didn't want to write that off as mere compulsiveness.

All right! The symbols danced on the page. He froze them by an effort of will. At the City of Angels—the name was a gesture of timid defiance, of course, on a par with a boy thumbing his nose at an adult whose back was turned —there had been this extraordinary instrusion. Words like "extraordinary" were losing their force. Lately you didn't even hear people say as they had used, "The Age of Miracles is not past." Now they said, with a wry shrug, "A of M!"—and that was its own explanation.

Canfield had arrived and found people jammed, physically jammed, in the exit doorway, and sprawled all over the low dais leading to it, dropped where the panic sprays caught them. And crushed under a table, the weirdo. And on top of the table, the man the manager believed to have been the target of the weirdo's interest. And on the floor nearby two girls and a man who had completed this particular party.

The man lying on the upturned table was called Dennis Radcliffe.

Waldron frowned. The name rang a distant bell. But he couldn't place it immediately. He wasted no time trying to puzzle it out—he could have the records checked easily enough.

The manager said Radcliffe had gone wild and started to hurl things: bottles, knives, crockery. But he hadn't seen what happened after that because of the rush for the exit and the need to turn on his gas-sprays.

So Canfield had closed out the place, of course, and taken all the hundred and forty names of clients and waiters and other staff by a slow process of searching pockets and purses for identity papers, and had brought here the people most directly involved: the manager, the bouncer and doorkeeper he suspected of lying, Radcliffe and the rest of his party, the weirdo himself, and half a dozen people picked at random to give corroborative evidence. A thorough job. Now it was three-ten A.M., and Waldron felt his vitality at such a low ebb he hated the prospect of sifting through the data Canfield had meticulously assembled.

But it was going to have to be done.

Where the hell do you start on a thing like this?

He shut the notebook and thumbed switches on his desk

intercom in the hope that it might have started working again by itself. It hadn't, and no one would be in to fix it before nine. He repressed the urge to throw it at the wall and got out of his chair.

The basement, white-tiled and forbidding, always put him in mind of a public toilet. There was something of the same stench about it, too, when the cells were full. Under harsh lights some of those arrested tonight moaned in their sleep; others, thinking even trying to sleep was futile, sat on hard benches and stared at nothing, eyes rimmed red with weariness. The people from the City of Angels were still unconscious for the most part, and lay like morgue-delivered corpses on the benches and floors in the end three cells.

At Waldron's appearance the men at the desk facing the cells glanced up. There were Rodriguez, the duty sergeant, Dr. Morello, one of the regular police surgeons, and Canfield, who glowered and bared his teeth.

Controlling his movements deliberately, Waldron descended the last few steps and held out the notebook. "I'm sorry I snapped at you, Canfield," he said. "Tired, I guess." He planted an elbow on the corner of the desk.

Canfield accepted the notebook and said nothing.

"Well, doc?" Waldron went on, his voice brittle. "What brings you here—the City of Angels affair, is it?"

Morello, whose eyelids were puffy and whose hair was uncombed, was writing out a report with the stylo chained to the desk in front of Rodriguez, and the chain was hampering. After favoring it with a muttered curse, he said, "Sure, they dragged me out to look at this weirdo. Could have waited until morning. Any fool could have seen he was dead."

"Did you say 'any fool'?" Canfield inquired in a tone as light as a caress. And when the doctor didn't respond, he went on, "I did what the regulations say! If you don't like being woken at two A.M., you don't have to have a police card. Want us to revoke it?"

Morello grimaced. "What the hell difference does it make if I get my patients from the police or pick 'em up off the street?" he said sourly. "Same color blood, same broken bones whichever way." Completing the last line of his scribbled report, he signed with a flourish and pushed the paper towards Rodriguez.

"Anybody got a cigarette?" he added. "I forgot mine."

"Here." Waldron proffered a pack. "I didn't realize the weirdo was dead, by the way."

"He wasn't when we brought him here," Canfield supplied. "He died about ten minutes before I came to see you. I'd have told you if I'd had the chance."

Ignoring the gibe, Waldron turned to Morello. "So what killed him? The things Radcliffe threw? The table falling on him?"

The doctor shrugged. "Contributory, maybe." He drew on his cigarette, closing his eyes momentarily as though to drown consciousness in the smoke. "But I doubt if you have a murder charge. Cerebral hemmorhage, far as I can tell. A whole slew of ruptured blood-vessels. His eyes are like cherries. My guess when they open up the skull at the autopsy, his brain will look like it's been stirred with an eggbeater." He uttered the similes with gloomy relish.

Uncomfortable, Waldron noticed that a woman in the cell directly opposite the desk was listening, her mouth slack, her eyes wide, and that now she was shuddering and licking her lips like a spectator at a *grand guignol* show. He decided not to look at her again.

"O.K.," he said. "Who was he? Anything known?"

"No papers on him," Canfield said. "Nothing. Wearing rags. Looked like he'd been through hell."

"No tattoo marks or anything like that, either." Morello spoke through a yawn. "Body covered in contusions a day or two old, plus fresh ones probably due to what got thrown at him. No major scars."

"Take his prints, then," Waldron said. "Have him cosmeticized and get some as-in-life pictures. Any hope of photographing the retinal patterns, doc?"

"Take the retinas out at the autopsy," Morello said. "His eyes are too messy to do a proper job through the corneas. I told you—they're like cherries."

"A lot of trouble," Rodriguez grumbled. "For a weirdo!"

Waldron didn't comment.

"Shouldn't be too much sweat." Morello yawned again, more widely. "Got one unusual thing about him. Mirror-image lay-out. Heart on the wrong side, large lobe of the liver on the wrong side, all the way down the line. Shouldn't be surprised if he's one of a pair of identical twins."

"Ah-hah!" Waldron said. "Got that, Chico?"

"It's in the report," Rodriguez grunted.

"So that's finish for me," Morello said. He picked up his bag from beside the desk. "Don't bother me too early in the morning. He's in freeze, he won't rot before the afternoon. And I'm short on sleep."

When his footsteps had died away on the echoing staircase, Waldron beckoned Canfield and walked over to the cells where the unconscious people from the City of Angels were lying.

"Which is Radcliffe?" he asked.

"That's him." Canfield pointed out a dark-haired man in very expensive clothes. Even in his drugged stupor his rather swarthy face wore a look of remembered terror. Waldron spoke to avoid thinking about the reason for that expression.

"We know something about him, don't we? I'm sure I've heard the name before."

"Could be, but not because we ever booked him here. He's the famous Den Radcliffe. Not a nice guy. Free trader, spends most of his time over with Governor Grady. They told us from the West Coast he'd been seen out of Grady's territory. Maybe you spotted the name on the teletype."

Not a nice guy! Hell of a mealy-mouthed way to put it! And anyway, what right did a Canfield have to dismiss such a man as his inferior? More gutsy than a Canfield, at least: not content to lie down in the shelter of the universal cheap pretenses. ...

"Want we should start with him?" Canfield proposed—eager, perhaps, to shift this living reminder of the plight of the world from under the roof they presently shared. Waldron had intended to leave Radcliffe until later anyway; hearing Canfield's tone, he felt the decision gilded with a vaneer of malicious pleasure.

"No, I'll start with the manager and his staff, and the people you picked up for corrobs. I'll have Radcliffe and the party who were with him after I've got the general picture from the ones who weren't directly involved."

For a moment he thought Canfield was going to raise objections. But he merely shrugged and called Rodriguez to open the first cell.

III

Appeared out of thin air. Looked around and spotted Radcliffe. Walked straight towards him—no, more kind of *plodded,* like he had weights tied to his ankles. Said something. Things were thrown. Panic. And oblivion. No, never saw him before. No idea who he might have been. Anyway, how to tell when his face was plastered with mud?

By the time he had picked through a dozen substantially identical stories, Waldron was regretting his petty desire to extend Canfield like a man on the rack. When Radcliffe was finally shown into the office he studied him with unconcealed curiosity. Radcliffe returned it with interest, his gaze lingering a long while on the hand-altered map pinned to the wall before he obeyed Waldron's invitation to come and sit down.

"You're Dennis W. Radcliffe, that right?" Waldron said.

"Right." Radcliffe crossed his legs. "Mind if I smoke?"

"Go ahead." Waldron turned the pedestal mike on the desk a little more towards the other's mouth. "This interview is being—"

"Recorded and may subsequently be used in evidence," Radcliffe interrupted wearily. "I've been through this sort of drill before."

"Have you had the full treatment?" Waldron countered. "The man you threw the table at is dead."

For a moment a wary flicker showed in Radcliffe's face. It vanished, and he was shrugging. "So? The panic sprays were on. Between inhalation and unconsciousness there's a period when a man isn't necessarily responsible for his actions."

Neat. Waldron took a cigarette for himself, wondering what set a Radcliffe so far apart from a Canfield.

"Are you making a charge?" Radcliffe added.

"Not yet. Do you wish legal representation?"

"Why should I, before you make a charge?"

"Yes or no, please!"

"Not yet—and I quote." Radcliffe grinned without mirth.

Waldron let it go at that. "Particulars, then. Age, birthplace, current address, permanent domicile, profession."

"Born Minneapolis. Age forty." Waldron had imagined him five years younger. "Hotel White Condor, suite 215. And I'm a free trader with a permanent domicile just outside Gradyville, but I don't believe you recognize the existence of such a place."

Defiance flavored the last words. Waldron extended his hand. "Documents?"

"They impounded them downstairs."

Waldron cursed inwardly. But Rodriguez must have done that to save time in compiling the written report; he couldn't complain.

"Right, let's go straight to the point. What's your version of this affair?"

It dovetailed exactly with the other accounts he had heard, but included one significant addition.

"He spoke to me," Radcliffe said. "He sounded crazy-mad. He said something like, 'Damn you, you did this to me!' I concluded he was insane and obviously dangerous."

"Are you qualified to pass judgment on people's sanity?"

"I deal with a wide and varied cross-section of the public in my profession," Radcliffe answered, without the bat of an eye.

"Go on."

"He made a move towards me which after his *seemingly* insane verbal attack I interpreted as hostile. To forestall an actual assault I threw a water-jug at him."

A pause. "Is that all?" Waldron pressed.

"When he kept coming, I threw something else—I forget what, because it was about then that the panic sprays came on. I made to raise the table as a barrier between us, I recall that, but I lost consciousness while doing so. I woke up on being revived in the cell downstairs."

Waldron probed further, but Radcliffe was too cagy to qualify what he had said. He switched the line of his approach.

"Who was this man? Had you seen him before?"

"Not to my knowledge. Of course, he was a weirdo, so—"

"What makes you so sure?"

"Jesus! I'll lay a bet that people in the restaurant who'd never before been within a hundred miles of one pegged him as soon as they laid eyes on him. And me, I've seen plenty."

Waldron hesitated. He said, "You describe yourself as a free trader. Define the term."

Oddly ill at ease for a moment, Radcliffe said, "I buy and sell—uh—rare artifacts."

"In the vicinity of the so-called alien city?"

Radcliffe lifted his chin half an inch. "Yes."

"That's where you've seen so many weirdos?"

"Of course." Radcliffe had apparently expected the questioning to turn overtly hostile; recognizing he was wrong, he sounded puzzled. "That's why I say I hadn't seen this character before to my knowledge. I didn't recognize him, I don't know his name or anything about him, but conceivably he may have seen me—uh—"

"On Grady's Ground?" Waldron suggested softly. His superiors wouldn't like that in the official record, but the hell with them. "What were you supposed to have done to him?"

"Heaven knows."

"You don't recall offending a weirdo lately, maybe?"

"I wouldn't even know how to go about it. They kind of lose touch with the world everyone else lives in, you know. Most of them are harmless, but some aren't. So I keep my distance from them."

"I see. So you'd never consciously met the guy, you don't know and won't guess what grudge he had against you, he made a crazy-sounding verbal attack on you which you thought was about to turn physical, and you were trying to drive him back when the panic sprays went on and you fell on him with the table. That correct?"

"That's the size of it."

Waldron studied the other for a few seconds, then gave a noncommittal grunt. "How about the other people at your table? Who were they?"

"The man's called Terry Hyson. A business contact of mine. I don't know anything about the girls except the blonde is called Sue and the brunette is called Maura. Terry provided them for the evening. I guess he had them from a supply agency."

"They charge?"

"Two-fifty." Radcliffe shrugged.

They would, of course. Someone like Radcliffe wasn't apt to get it any other way outside his home ground. As though Grady's dirt, rather than his own guts, were the significant thing. Abruptly Waldron found himself feeling angry on Radcliffe's behalf. He said, "O.K., I guess that's enough. If we want you again we'll trace you through Hyson or at your hotel. When do you plan to leave the city?"

"Not before the weekend, as things stand." If Radcliffe was surprised the interview had been so easy, he didn't show it.

"Fine. You can go." Waldron moved pencils randomly on his desk.

But Radcliffe didn't make to leave at once. His gaze roamed the office, coming to rest on the hemisphere map, at which he jerked a thumb.

"You haven't got it quite right."

"What do you mean?"

"This." Radcliffe rose and approached the map, laying his finger on the western edge of the black tongue-shaped outline defining Grady's Ground. "Goes forty-fifty miles further west here."

"Thanks for the information," Waldron muttered.

"You been out that way?" Radcliffe cocked his head.

"No."

"You should." He gave a crooked smile. "Some time when you get sick of making phony gestures in this smelly little room, come out and see me. I'm not hard to track down."

How the hell did he know? For a short eternity Waldron saw nothing but Radcliffe's eyes, and then he heard himself say, "I guess—yes, maybe I will. Maybe I will."

When the door closed, Waldron found he was sweating. His teeth were going to chatter if he didn't set his jaw hard. He looked towards the window. Dawn was breaking over the city.

He was kidding himself, worse than the Canfields of the world. Radcliffe had seen right through him in a few minutes. Sticking a map on the wall and thinking that was as far as honesty need go. . .

The door opened and the first girl came in. She was very pretty, with sleek dark hair braided to the back of her head with gold wire, but she looked peaked with cold. Not surprisingly. She wore a synsilk nightsuit of dark red tassels on net covering her left arm and breast, her belly and buttocks, and her right leg. *Two-fifty,* Waldron thought. *At that price I guess she can afford to shiver.*

"Sit down," he said. "Name?"

"Maura Knight." She dropped into the chair. "Got a cigarette?"

"No. Particulars?"

When she gave her profession as "secretary", he pounced. "So what are you charging Radcliffe—overtime?"

"Sure, overtime!" she snapped. "If you know girls who don't charge, they're probably rich!"

Waldron framed a retort, then sighed and changed his mind. It wasn't her fault that nowadays sex seemed to be bought and sold more often than given, as though along with its old ambitions the human race had abandoned any conception of love in the bright awful shadow of Earth's invaders.

He asked for her version of events, and she recited it in dull fatigued tones. Once again it tallied exactly, up to the point at which the weirdo spoke. And then a little life seemed to enter her; she sat forward on the chair, looking past him into memory, and her voice rose from its former colorless level to a pitch almost to be called passionate.

"He said something like, 'You did this to me, you damned bastard!' I looked at Den—I mean Radcliffe. I've never *seen* such a murderous look! He picked up this heavy jug and threw it, and that wasn't enough. The weirdo hadn't done anything and he still didn't do anything. He just kept glaring, his face full of hate. And Radcliffe threw a bottle, and it *smashed* on his head!" She closed her eyes and sank back. Staring at her, Waldron saw her swallow as though fighting the need to vomit.

"I tell you, I saw him smash the bottle on the guy's head. And then he threw anything else he could find, like a lunatic trying to ruin a doll. Plates, knives, anything. As though he'd gone completely berserk."

Waldron didn't say anything. But he wondered why she hated Radcliffe so, on such short acquaintance.

"He was trying to throw the whole damned *table* when the gas came on! Listen, why did he want to do that?" She opened her eyes again, this time wide with incredulity. "Sure, this weirdo looked revolting, but . . . but . . . Oh, I don't know much about these things, but I always thought a weirdo gets that way because he doesn't just sit around like everybody else letting himself be treated like vermin by the—the whatever they are. He's someone who's tried to do something, even if he has wound up crazy. I think he was telling the truth. I think he wanted to get his own back because Radcliffe had done something terrible to him. Cheated him, maybe. How do the free traders get their stuff, anyway? Do they really scavenge for it, or do they leave the dirty work to other people and kick them out if they take one risk too many and lose their minds?"

"Shut up," Waldron said coldly. He was taken aback, not only to hear her uttering comments on this level, but also to find that he half-wanted her to continue. Even to talk about defiance was better than ignoring reality altogether.

"You met Radcliffe for the first time last evening, didn't you?" he demanded.

She gave a sullen nod.

"Then you'd better think twice before jumping to slanderous conclusions, hadn't you?"

33

She was ice-calm suddenly. "Weren't you just trying to insinuate me into your records as a professional prostitute? After an even shorter acquaintance!"

He was in acute danger of losing his temper, Waldron realized, and over people he didn't give a damn about at that. He told her to go. Shivering, she moved towards the door. Just before going out, she gave him a glance sharp with contempt.

She has no right. . . . But the thought would not complete.

When he had spoken to Hyson and the other girl, Susan Vey, he felt physically and emotionally drained. He could risk napping for the rest of his tour if Canfield had nothing more for him—but to find out whether that was so, he would have to go down to the basement again. *Damn* that intercom.

As he turned the corner of the stairway and came in sight of the cells, the fact that some of the prisoners had broken out of their apathy and were staring towards the desk told him something must be wrong. He hurried down the next half-dozen steps and could then see for himself: Canfield and Rodriguez each holding Radcliffe by one arm, while facing him, her cheeks very white, her lower lip puffy and a trickle of blood creeping out of the corner of her mouth, Maura Knight still held up her hands defensively as though to ward him off.

IV.

Waldron felt as though the world were throwing events at his head the way Radcliffe had bombarded the weirdo *(had* it been like a madman smashing a doll?) and it was making him giddy. It seemed when he spoke that plates of hard dry skin were flaking around his mouth.

"What the hell is going on?" he demanded.

Canfield and Rodriguez let Radcliffe go. The trader took a step back and shrugged his coat into place around his shoulders, his expression stony as a statue's. Canfield jerked a thumb at him.

"I imagine Radcliffe is going back in the cage," he said. "I never saw a man hit a woman like that before. Did he break any teeth?" he added to Maura.

She shook her head numbly. Feeling the blood on her chin, she wiped at it with the back of her hand.

"What for?" Waldron said, addressing Radcliffe.

"She didn't expect to find me waiting for her," Radcliffe snarled. "Thought she could slip out of here and sneak off home. But I want value for the two-fifty I gave her!"

"You can have the money!" the girl cried. "You—"

"I want what I paid for! Come across, or I'll help myself. It's up to you!"

"Be quiet!" Canfield rapped. "I don't know what the hell you do on Grady's Ground, and I don't care. But what

37

you're going to do here is head back into a cell the moment she says the word."

"Listen, you wooden-headed angel-chaser!" Radcliffe began, balling a fist.

"Hold it!" Waldron barked. "You! What's your name? You, Maura! Want to swear out an assault charge?"

"No, I don't want to have to see him again, even in court. He can take his dirty money. Now I have some idea how he gets it I'd rather be rid of it before I catch—"

"Chico!" Waldron exclaimed, and Rodriguez clamped down on Radcliffe's arm before it could deliver a second punch. "Take your money, Radcliffe. Count yourself lucky she doesn't want her pound of flesh. Free traders aren't any too popular around here."

The anger drained from Radcliffe all at once. He relaxed, eyes on Waldron. "I guess you're right," he admitted. "You take the money off her, then. If I go any closer I'm apt to forget my good manners."

Where the hell could she be carrying money in that outfit, anyway? Oh: the gold-braided hair on the back of her head was a chignon. She lifted it off, produced the bills; Canfield returned them to Radcliffe.

"Now—out," he grunted. "And remember what the lieutenant said. You're *damned* lucky."

"Aren't you going to give me a head start over him?" Maura said. "You heard him say he didn't want the money, he'd rather take what he paid for."

Radcliffe grinned. Waldron caught the expression as it came and went, but couldn't be sure whether it was wry or —what to call it? Vicious? He passed his hand across his face.

"Send her home in a squad car, goddamn it!" he ordered. "Anything for the sake of peace and quiet!"

In the main lobby he paused, looking out through the

doors at the early-morning street. A cleansing cart was crawling by, its huge vacuum mouths slurping up their diet of litter, its hind end giving back a flood of detergent and water like urine. His mind seemed to switch off, and minutes passed without his realizing. Then there came a tap on his shoulder.

"I appreciate what you did for me there, lieutenant," Radcliffe said. "Back home, I guess I'm in the habit of doing as I see fit and to hell with the consequences. It isn't often that someone can talk me around as neatly as you just did. I'll settle matters some other way, or if I can't, what the hell? Either way, I promise it won't concern you."

He drew back half a pace and looked Waldron over with a searching stare.

"Don't forget what I said, will you? I'm accustomed to making snap judgments, you know—I have to, because all the time people are wandering on to the Ground, and I have to decide usually on the basis of a five-minute chat whether it's worth hiring them or letting them go to somebody else. And I've made my mind up about you. I have a security problem. You could handle it the way I want. Give me the chance to do you a favor back—come out where things actually happen. You said you very well might."

Had he really said so? The memory of his own words came back to Waldron from infinitely long ago. He gave a listless nod.

"Great. Take your time to think it over, of course. But my guess is that you've already had your bellyful of this play-acting. See you shortly!"

With a smile and a wave Radcliffe headed for the exit, while Waldron returned to his office.

Like a lunatic trying to smash a doll. . . ?

He had thought of laying his head on the desk and trying to doze away the last hour of his shift, but that was out of the question, for he could hear the sounds of the building coming to daytime life—office-cleaning machines going up and down the service racks between floors, coffee-and-rolls trolleys rattling down the corridors for the overnight staff. One more mortal hour before he could leave. Of course, this had been a good night in one sense —no shootings, no arson, no gang-rumbles or major riots . . .

How were things in the old days?

The coffee trolley stopped at his door and hooted. He collected his ration. Sipping it, puffing at the latest of too many cigarettes tonight, he stared at the map. Radcliffe had claimed that Grady's western boundary reached forty or fifty miles further out. If he made the change, nobody would notice. Or—well, they might, but they'd think of it as a gibe, not an attempt to face the truth. *De jure,* they would say, the USA is still the USA, Canada is still Canada. *De Facto,* of course—but that's not exactly our fault, is it?

Where would we have got to by now if the aliens hadn't come?

He remembered the beginning with fearful vividness. No one had known what was really happening, of course —they'd taken it for a mere crisis in human affairs. Internal, so to say. (Almost funny, that. Like a cerebral hemorrhage. It occurred to him that the reason why Morello had been so pleased with his comparison of the weirdo's eyes to cherries was that a kind of dark cherry was called a Morello.)

With casual simultaneity, all fissionable material on the planet had been exploded with an efficiency ranging from eight to eighteen percent conversion. Every missile and bomber base; every bomb in flight; every nuclear power station and every refinery where the stocks exceeded a couple of kilograms had mushroomed into fire. It was a day and a half before the survivors knew it wasn't war. With the exception of those who would have started such a war. They knew. But for that day and a half they withheld their knowledge out of panic.

During that time something became clear which previously governments and general staffs had preferred to play down, since they still existed in a fantasy world where concepts like "victory" and "conquest" were meaningful. Modern industrial society was like a watch. To drop a single pinch of sand into the works was to ruin it. And this was no pinch of sand—it was a truckload. The anti-missile missiles, ranked in sets of forty per million population, naturally did the most damage; each had a warhead designed to knock down an enemy rocket on a seven-mile near miss. The bombers and ICBM's were in comparatively isolated districts, or aboard submarines far out to sea, while the Minutemen and other city-wreckers wasted their blast on their underground silos.

It wasn't the explosions, or the gigantic fires—worst on the West Coast, where they swept thousands of square miles at the end of a dry summer—or even the fallout which caused the disruption of North America. It was the people who fled from the fires, abandoning their homes and their jobs; it was the plagues which ran through refugee camps when city-dwellers drank bad water; it was the National Guardsmen and hastily sworn-in armed deputies who fought pitched battles to turn back swarms of metropolitan fugitives made mindless by terror when they reached the outskirts of smaller towns. In Europe things were infinitely worse, because the giant opposed armies went into battle like machines turned on by the nuclear explosions, and ravaged both Germanies, most of Czechoslovakia and parts of other countries before it was possible to switch them off.

There was a time—according to what event one chose to mark its ending, one said it lasted weeks or months—during which the planet churned like an overset beehive, and nobody seemed able to think far enough ahead to restore any organization. It was in this period that the alien cities were built.

One said: "alien city". And was no wiser.

Bewildered governments brought their immediate problems under control, arranged emergency food supplies, drafted doctors to the rash of refugee camps, charted the fallout zones, and learned with relief and dismay that the calamity was as worldwide as the distribution of fissionables. It was in Israel and India, Chile and China. (Inevitably, though, the countries where weapons had been readied suffered worst.)

Also they learned that in the north middlewest of the USA almost touching the Canadian border, in western Brazil, in Russia a short distance east of the Urals, in Australia's Nullabor Plain, and in the Antarctic, there were . . . strangenesses. From the air they were seen as distorted five-pointed stars, glowing translucent, vaster than any city yet seeming to be single buildings—if they were buildings. There was energy in them; the radio bands crackled with static, electrical storms gathered around them, and occasionally a shattering noise was heard, though such phenomena dwindled and eventually ceased. Within the boundaries of these places—misty, sometimes nearly opaque and sometimes glass-clear, constantly radiating unpredictable patterns of color—could be discerned shining entities. Question mark.

People thought: invasion. And within a few more weeks moved against the intruders. It was still impossible to assemble more than two or three kilograms of fissionable material anywhere; that was tried and proved. But they sent armies with conventional bombs and rockets, and

42

thought in terms of seige, and were repulsed with madness.

What it was due to—poison gas, telepathic bombardment, mass hypnotism, a virus—no one knew. But the armies dispatched against the shining cities reached a certain point which might not even be in sight of their target, and then mutinied and turned back. They raved across the countryside wrecking, looting, burning—fire gave them especial pleasure and they would stand watching a haystack blaze until it was almost all ash, then pour gasoline on it to enjoy another few minutes of flame. Overhead, planes released their bombs anywhere but on the alien cities, then sought a funeral pyre in a human city or, most favored, an oilfield.

It became impossible to pretend to the continuance of national government anywhere near the alien-controlled areas. You couldn't tell whether the army battalion which came to invest your town was under orders from Washington—or Moscow, come to that, for the terror reigned everywhere—to protect you, or was waiting with lunatic glee for night to fall so that your home might be set ablaze with maximum spectacle.

Little by little things settled towards a semblance of normality. No further assaults were made on the alien cities. It was in their vicinity that chaos lasted longest. Realizing that no government would dare send in troops to reestablish authority for fear of adding to the toll of those rendered insane, a few men saw their chance, and snatched at it. In Russia, the man who emerged as ruler of the no-man's-land was called Buishenko; in Australia it was Villiers-Hart; in Brazil, Neveira; and in North America the self-styled "Governor" Grady.

These had fought other, less astute rivals to seize the reins of effective power in the lull between the extremity of the crisis and the present. It did not seem to matter if humans squabbled among themselves in plain sight of the alien cities; the madness only struck if they actually contemplated an attack.

Like speculative builders erecting apartments on the San Andreas fault, like peasants farming the slopes of a volcano, others joined them and accepted their arbitrary rule. They were lured by greed.

For there were what Radcliffe had called "rare artifacts"—the garbage, perhaps, of the nonhuman beings who had descended on Earth. They hinted at fantastic new principles, undiscovered laws of nature, energy-states which were neither matter nor radiation. Instantly commercial and governmental interests set to squabbling and bargaining for them. In the States all that were found were nominally federal property, but the decree was a nullity. So, trading like vermin on the refuse of a higher species, Grady and his counterparts enjoyed a tenuous security.

But it took guts, didn't it, to perch there on the volcano's lip, trying to snatch meager clues to the nature of the invaders? Most of humanity, ran a phrase which seemed apposite to Waldron, was writhing like a snake with a broken back. The free traders were at least the equal of rats . . . also a species preying on the leavings of a higher one.

His aimless musing was interrupted. The door opened to reveal Canfield, extremely weary. He said, "About the weirdo—" And waved a sheet of teletype paper.

"Yes?" Waldron stirred. "Have you identified him?"

"Not exactly. But you remember what Morello said— he might be one of a pair of identical twins, seeing his body is laid out mirror-fashion. So when Washington said they didn't have his prints on file, I said to try reversing them."

"Ah, hell!" Waldron said with incipient scorn. "Not even twins have identical prints, you know that."

Canfield bristled. "Haven't you put me down enough for one night, even yet?" he snapped. "Not that I give a shit anyhow. I *found* his twin."

"*What?*"

"See for yourself." Canfield dropped the paper on the desk. "A guy called Corey Bennett. Works for the Federal Scientific Service. The match-up of the prints is *exact*."

A cold shiver invaded Waldron's spine. "But it's impossible," he said faintly.

"A of M!" Canfield grunted, and marched out.

V

"Are you *sure* it isn't a trap?" Jespersen said again.

Orlando Potter glanced around. All lights were out on the bridge of the jet-driven Coast Guard launch, bar the shaded lamp over the navigation table, but the northern summer sky was bright enough to show faces. Not for the first time he regretted bringing along the rangy Swedish-born physicist as "scientific advisor"—hell, what use was human science where the aliens were concerned? Irritation embrittling his voice, he said, "I've *told* you! We know beyond a shadow of doubt they're desperate. Isn't that proved by what they did for Congreve?"

Not turning his head, continuing to stare across the smooth shield of the sea, Congreve gave a cynical grunt. "I sometimes think you've stopped regarding Russians as human, doctor! They're as capable of being frightened as you and I. And believe me, they *are* frightened."

Improbably out of place in this stark, almost warlike setting—blonde hair hanging loose, makeup impeccable, her only concession to the task in hand being her choice of a jerkin-and-pants suit in dark suede rather than one of her regular bright and revealing costumes—Greta Delarue tossed in one of the innocent-seeming questions that often made it impossible even for Potter to tell which way her mind was running . . . and she had been his mistress for six months now.

"Obviously, Mike. But which are they more scared of: the aliens, or Buishenko?"

Congreve didn't reply immediately. During the pause Potter found himself studying the spy for the latest of many, many times, struggling to discern from some outward clue whether his loyalty had been undermined.

Congreve was still in Russian clothes: the green zip-fronted jacket, the black pants with elasticized cuffs and baggy calves reminiscent of Cossack breeches which had been fashionable at the latest period when there were still fashions to engage the attention of Russia's prosperous new class. His Moscow-styled hair was growing out of its intended neatness, but since his return he had hardly had time for such minor problems as getting it trimmed.

By their tens of thousands, Potter thought, *men in such clothes are falling under Buishenko's sway. He's gobbling up Russia like a new Khan of the Golden Horde. Did any of his agents get to Congreve?*

And if so—how?

"I wish," Congreve said finally, "people would get cured of this contempt for spies! I'm a damned good spy, and proud of it. I've been and out of the Soviet Union for more than eight years, and they still weren't sure I was a foreigner even when they decided to make their approach. They took a gamble. I spent a full week checking before I came into the open. And they sent me out through Austria by one of their own routes, on a government pass with ten thousand rubles and the message. In my judgment they're equally scared of both the aliens and Buishenko because you can't separate them. If it hadn't been for the aliens he could never have achieved power. You haven't seen what he's doing to Russia. I have!"

Abandoning his contemplation of the sea at last, he turned. "That's not like Grady's Ground, for God's sake— it's not just a kind of make-believe Gold Rush enclave!

50

It's a cancer of barbarism, and it's spreading like a forest fire!"

"I only wish"—Potter heard his own voice with vague surprise—"that we knew exactly what we're supposed to be waiting for."

"It could be any of half a dozen things." Greta shrugged. "My guess is an alien device in operating condition. If I'm right, it would be worth much greater risks than what we're actually taking."

Jespersen snorted. He was a tall man, and anxiety had wasted him until his skin hung loose on his bones. His hair, which had been light brown before the coming of the aliens, had turned to silver and started to fall away almost by the handful. "Going by what they told Congreve, we can't be certain of anything. A lot of gibberish and double-talk, that's what I call it."

"Here we go again," muttered Congreve. "I was hoping that scientists might be a bit less hidebound than politicians, or my own people, but it seems I was wrong . . . No, Dr. Jesperson, it wasn't gibberish! It made perfectly good sense. They've managed to get their hands on something which Buishenko will stop at nothing to get back. They can't keep it in the Soviet Union because the country is just tumbling around their ears. They can't take it out westwards because Central Europe is impassable on land and anyhow Buishenko controls half their surviving anti-aircraft guns and missiles and any plane they tried to put into the sky would probably be shot down. There was no point in taking it out northwards; that's a dead end, and it would probably be stuck in Finland until Buishenko marched in there, too. But they did think they could get it out through Vladivostok and if I could arrange safe custody for it on delivery they'd make the attempt." His voice was tinged with weariness. Potter wondered how often he had already recited this story—under hypnosis, under drugs, his mind being probed to its roots in search of any hint of treason.

The radio mounted over the navigation table came to life, and the naval commander sitting there answered without taking his eyes from the radar screen.

"Harlequin, Harlequin—pawn to rook four!"

"Columbine," a distant voice said. "Queen to queen one, check."

"They're coming!" Potter said under his breath, and moved to peer over the commander's shoulder. At the helm the captain—also naval, not a Coast Guard officer —demanded to know whether they had a fix yet.

The commander shut off the radio briefly to say he had a blip at the extreme limit of range, but nothing definite, and relayed similar information in verbal code to the headquarters ship referred to as Columbine. It was a curious makeshift fleet they had mounted to carry out this operation: after the worldwide destruction of fissionables, the Navy was left without its aircraft carriers, without its cruisers and destroyers, without its nuclear submarines . . . "Columbine" had been a lowly pre-atomic sub-chaser, cocooned and due for the scrapyard.

An eternal pause followed, during which all their eyes focused achingly on the commander's face, eerily lit by the shaded yellow lamp above, the green glow of the radar below.

"Harlequin," he said finally. "Discovered check—very neat. King's knight to queen five."

"If anybody's listening," Jespersen grumbled, "they'll be damned sure we're not just playing chess to pass the time!"

"The moves are legal!" Congreve snapped. "It may not be a good game, but it is a game! Damn it, I spent two weeks working up the code, didn't I?"

Jespersen scowled but fortunately forebore to answer.

"What the hell. . . ?" the commander said, half to himself. "Either there's something wrong with the radar, or . . . No, it's really there."

"What?" the captain snapped.

"I don't know. Not quite what we were expecting, that's definite. The range is closing on every sweep, and the speed—" The commander checked a printed list pasted beside the radar screen. "Christ. It says sixty-five knots. Are you sure we're expecting a watergoing vessel, Mr. Congreve?"

"That's what I was told," Congreve answered. "I guess they might have managed to get their hands on a plane after all, but at the time they were quite definite. In any case that's too slow for a plane, isn't it?"

"A helicopter, wave-hopping to keep below following radar?" Greta offered.

"Possible," the commander conceded. "But could we have silence now, please?"

He resumed his coded contact with the headquarters ship.

Pointlessly, Potter, Greta and Jespersen formed up in a line to stare in the direction from which the Russian craft was approaching, though they well knew nothing was to be seen as yet.

"How soon will it be close enough for us to spot it?" Jespersen muttered, fingering a pair of binoculars on a strap around his chicken-thin neck.

"Depends what size it is, doesn't it?" Congreve answered mockingly, and the tall Swede flushed.

The voice from Columbine muttered, "Uh . . . now that the . . . ? Oh yeah. Castle king side, check and double-check on the next move. With the queen's knight. Better watch it."

"What's that supposed to mean?" Jespersen growled.

"They're being followed," Potter said. "Right, Congreve?"

The spy nodded, gazing anxiously up into the twilit sky.

Their own vessel's "counter-move" Potter failed to catch. That didn't matter, though, for the next statement from headquarters was about pawn taking pawn, and from somewhere astern a string of half a dozen glowing objects crossed the zenith like shooting stars in reverse. Tension grew. Then . . .

"Got them!" Greta said with uncharacteristic excitement. Something had shone red on the horizon and faded instantly.

"What was it, could you tell?" Potter asked the commander in a hushed voice.

"Air pursuit," the officer answered equally quietly. "I don't know why the shots came from astern, though. We're supposed to have a couple of conventional-missile ships ahead of us—"

"Guard your queen!" Columbine said sharply, and in the same moment Jespersen, binoculars raised, let out a muffled exclamation.

Even without glasses Potter could not only see the thing rushing towards them, but recognize that there was something peculiar about its design as soon as its movement attracted his eye. "What is it?" he exclaimed.

"I think it's a *Red Whale*," Congreve said.

Potter struggled to make sense of an incongruous lopsided form half in, half out of the water. "What's a *Red Whale*, for God's sake?"

"Hydro-aerofoil," Greta said unexpectedly. "Four turbines, two underwater foils, two wings. Experimental. Meant for high-speed transit in the China Sea. If it's only doing sixty-five knots it's loafing. Its design speed is a hundred and ten."

"Shut up!" the captain ordered, and Potter realized

they must have missed some vital exchange with Columbine, for the whine of the engines had sharpened noticeably.

The commander gave a nod, and the captain's hand shot to the power control. He barked at his passengers. "Hold on to something! Here we go!"

They all grabbed at the metal rails which ringed the bridge, and in the same second the pursuit launch took off: bump-bump-slap on three consecutive waves and then up on its foils and dead steady, like a limousine on a concrete road. The plume of the jets stretched astern for a hundred yards.

"Something wrong?" Potter demanded.

"Very," the captain confirmed. "There's a 'copter up there with infrared cameras and an electron-multiplier. Pilot reports one wing shot off the Russian—ah—vessel, one engine stopped to balance the drag, and a nose-down attitude. Must have been hit before we took out the plane that was chasing her."

"I can see the damage!" Jespersen burst out. "How is it still afloat?"

Potter seized a spare pair of binoculars from an overhead rack he had only just noticed. Jespersen was right. Not only was one wing of the awkward craft missing; there was a hole in the hull, and water was slapping up towards it.

The radio emitted an abrupt blast of frantic Russian. Congreve was translating before he was asked.

"They're in great danger—at this speed the hydrofoils hit a critical resonance and make the hull shiver—if they reduce speed they'll drop and water will come through the hole—if they go faster they'll tip over because of the missing wing! They must ditch as soon as possible! If we can come close and pick them out of the water flash a light three times."

Instantly the captain hit the main deck-lights switch. The whole of the boat stood out in sudden glaring whiteness.

"Look!" Greta whispered.

The monstrous, misshapen Russian vessel had swung broadside in a terrific swirl of spray. Something detached from it: a jettisoned hatch, leaving a bright oblong on the hull. A figure tumbled out. Another. Another. Like toys.

"But why on the turn like . . . ?" the captain said to no one in particular. And then: "Oh, of course. Centrifugal force—toss them clear of the wake."

"Whoever's at the helm knows his business," the commander said soberly.

The captain dropped the launch back to slow ahead and the uneven rocking of the waves. A searchlight from her bow swept the water and picked up three bobbing heads in quick succession.

The *Red Whale* completed a hundred-and-eighty degree turn and slammed back on its original track. One more doll-like figure dived out—and a heartbeat later the craft dipped, dug its nose in, and shattered to pieces with a grinding roar.

"Made it!" Potter cried, beside himself with uncontrollable excitement.

"The hell you say," Greta snapped. Potter gave her a blank stare. She repeated: "The hell you say! Whatever they were bringing, they didn't push it through the escape hatch, did they? I only saw men going into the water, not taking anything with them—which means the reason for all our trouble is at the bottom of the Pacific!"

VI

In the excitement of watching the brilliant maneuver carried out by the Russian helmsman, Potter had completely forgotten about the consignment they were expecting; he had been concentrating on the figures pitching out of the emergency door. And for the next several minutes too much was happening to permit quiet thought. He comforted himself with the idea that perhaps the precious object—whatever it was—might be very small, pocket-sized . . . though that hardly matched the scale of the alien cities or the mysterious entities which had been glimpsed within them.

All four of the survivors' life-jackets had inflated properly, and although one of them appeared to be unconscious and they were widely scattered, there was no need for excessive haste. Potter stood by on the afterdeck while muscular sailors operated a retrieval device, a cross between a grapnel and a lasso designed to catch a floating body in a padded ring.

First to be rescued was a grossly fat man whose life-jacket would barely fasten over his chest. He was coughing helplessly from a lungful of water, and had still not recovered from his convulsions when the second followed: a pale man with a spade-shaped brown beard salted with gray.

This one was in sufficiently good shape to stand unaided

as he reached the deck, and even to bow his thanks to the sailor who had hauled him up. Congreve addressed him in Russian and at once had both his hands clasped fervently.

"What's he saying?" Potter whispered.

"His name's Alexei Zworykin. Medical doctor. Says he was never so glad in his life as when he saw us flash our lights."

"What's his reason for coming along?"

"I haven't asked that yet." Congreve resumed his questioning.

Number three to be fished up was the unconscious one. The instant he came into view at the gunwale, limp as a dead fish, Zworykin forgot everything and dashed forward with an oath. Dropping to his knees, he checked the newcomer's pulse and rolled back his eyelids. He uttered an impatient order to Congreve.

"We must get him below at once," the ex-spy relayed. "He has a very frail constitution."

"I can believe that," Potter agreed. The white impassive face showing above the collar of the life-jacket was somehow. . .wrong. Deformed. The features were in a false relationship: forehead too low, eyes too far apart, mouth slack and idiotic.

"He's diabetic," Congreve said. "Also has a skin disease and something else—a medical term—I can't remember the English for."

"Well, if he's here presumably he's important," Potter grunted. "Get them below and see the doctor's given whatever he needs."

He turned to see how the fat man was, and found Greta and Jespersen in halting conversation with him, their Russian badly accented and full of struggling pauses. Even so, Potter—who had not even a nodding acquaintance with the language—felt envious.

"Who is he?" he inquired.

He had meant the question for Great, but it was Jespersen who replied, with thinly veiled contempt. "Don't you recognize him? Pavel Abramovitch, their Minister of Science!"

Of course! Potter damned himself for not identifying the man, but somehow, even after what Congreve had reported, he hadn't expected anyone of this eminence to be with the party. Abramovitch was no chair-polishing career politician, either—he had already been an Academician of the USSR with a noteworthy research record when one of the periodical Kremlin reshuffles brought him into the Supreme Soviet.

He was about to request a formal introduction when there came an exclamation from behind, and he swung around.

Number four of the survivors was climbing aboard without the aid of rescue apparatus. Sleek black hair running-wet framed a square Slavic face; on sallow skin red lips showed like an open wound. A woman? Well—unmistakably!

In excellent English she said, "Thank you very much. I was hoping we could get all the way under our own power, which was why we asked for a jet-propelled boat to meet us and ride into port together. But it was hard to evade the attacks because seawater is not my usual habitation!" She bestowed a sunny smile on everyone in view.

There was a moment of enduring astonishment. Potter ended it by moving forward, hand outstretched.

"Ah—I'm Orlando Potter," he said. "Theoretically I'm in charge. I'm deputy chairman of the Congressional Committee on Emergency Countermeasures, if that means anything to you."

"It would be like our commission on—" The girl snapped her fingers. "Oh, I don't know the English for that! I am Natasha Nikolaevna."

Her self-possession impressed Potter tremendously. He said, "You were the . . . the pilot of the ship?"

"I was steering, yes." A wry grimace. "But it was not what I am used to, you understand. I am a cosmonaut."

A cosmonaut! That word brought a rush of agonizing nostalgia to Potter: so many aborted dreams . . . Before he had framed a suitable comment, Greta came tapping him on the shoulder.

"Orlando, you must come and talk to Abramavitch. He has something important to say, but he won't tell anybody below government level." There was a hint of irritation in her voice. Potter made to excuse himself to the Russian girl and comply, but she shot an urgent question at him.

"How is Pitirim? Is he all right?"

"Do you mean the sick boy?" Potter found the words come automatically; on reflection the unconscious survivor had seemed very young, perhaps in his teens. "He's below with the doctor, being well looked after."

"I'm so glad," the girl exclaimed. "Any of the rest of us could have been lost, but I was afraid for Pitirim."

Why? What could make a mere boy—an apparent mental defective, at that—more important than the Minister for Science? But Potter had no chance to ask, for the captain called from the bridge.

"Mr. Potter, take everyone below, will you? We're getting underway, and even if we can't hit a hundred and ten knots there'll be a slight breeze here on deck."

A slight breeze, Potter repeated to himself. The pursuit launch was slicing the night at about forty-five knots now, and the wind-noise and the yammer of the turbines permeated the entire hull, making conversation in the cramped quarters amidships a matter of slow well-articulated shouting.

Congreve came to join them, and reported that Zworykin was wearing a comprehensive medical kit strapped around his body in a waterproof covering and didn't want anyone else to interfere while he attended to the unconscious Pitirim. He sat down next to Abramavitch; the fat man was at a worse disadvantage than the others when trying to talk above the noise, because his fit of coughing had left him hoarse. But anything he wanted to say would have to be relayed anyhow by Congreve or Natasha, and they were either side of him.

Potter caught Natasha's eye. "Please explain to Mr. Abramovitch who I am. And please tell him, too, that Dr. Jespersen is Associate Professor of Physics at the University of British Columbia and Miss Delarue is a senior executive of our Federal Scientific Service, so he can speak freely to all of us."

Natasha complied. Waiting for her to translate the reply, Potter found himself glancing at Greta. There was an unexpectedly sour expression on her lovely face. It couldn't possibly be jealousy, could it?

Yes, it could. For on reflection he realized it had made its appearance as they were coming below, when the captain had called from the bridge to compliment Natasha on her skilled handling of the *Red Whale*. He knew very well it was not to Greta's taste to have other women around who excelled her in anything, be it looks or ability.

She must be quite a girl, this cosmonaut. . . . I wonder how she feels about the aliens, whether she finds it possible to hate them. How many years of ambition, how much tough training, went to waste because of them? It will be long before another spaceship leaves this ravaged planet.

But he himself had long ago realized, to his surprise, that he did not hate the aliens because he could not. They were too foreign to his understanding. One might as well hate a bacterium, or a storm-cloud.

"He finds it difficult to talk," Natasha said now, turning

back to Potter. "His throat hurts. So please put your questions to me, and I will only translate them to him if I cannot answer. Is this O.K. by you?"

Imperfections were beginning to show in her generally astonishing English; that faintly archaic phrase was one. Nonetheless her accent was superb. Potter shaped his first query and was forestalled by Greta in a voice as bitter as aloes.

"Is there any point? You saved nothing from the wreck except yourselves."

"Please?" Natasha countered, eyes widening in puzzlement.

Potter scowled Greta into silence. Plainly she was still concerned that no alien device had been salvaged from the sunken boat, but there was nothing in the Russians' demeanor to suggest that they considered their venture a failure. On the contrary, they seemed in very good spirits.

"Miss—ah—Miss Nikolaevna," he said, "we ought to start with the full background to the story, you know. What Mr. Congreve was told didn't make it at all clear."

She checked rapidly with Abromovitch; on his confirmatory nod she leaned back and crossed her legs.

"Very well! First, you know what it is like in Russia now—there is Buishenko who has risen like a mad dog to the top of a pile of mad dogs, and his saboteurs and criminals are breaking up the organization of our state and fighting over the pieces. It is like a jungle! First there was only the part around the . . . the alien city, I think you call it in English. We are discouraged to call it that. Officially the name is 'energetic phenomenon'. But I myself am sure there are thinking creatures inside, much advanced over us.

"Well, it spread like a plague, you see. But we could not understand why Buishenko gained so much support. We have done much for our people, and believed them mainly loyal. It is in some way a superstition, but there is great love of Mother Russia. Of course he began with the remnants of the maddened leaderless armies we had sent against the . . . the aliens. Many thousands of them survived but had no organization until he enrolled them. Also many people joined him through fear, or for bribes, or to save their skins from his terrorist forces. But this could not be the whole of the story. There were still gapes, do you follow me? Ah—gapes. . .?"

"Gaps," Potter supplied.

"Thank you, yes. So we spied, and we sent commando forces into his territory, and we interrogated those we captured in battle against him, and it came out. Our government had done its best against the aliens, and they spat on our petty achievements. Buishenko had done what we could not manage, so in the face of the terrible strange threat people turned willingly to him."

She paused impressively, looking from face to face.

"What our captives said was this: Buishenko had found a way to enter and leave the alien city at will, and obtained many strange marvelous objects as proof."

"You mean"—Potter heard his voice shaking—"he didn't go out of his mind?" In memory, scores of movie films showing those who had tried to enter the city in North America and been rendered instantly insane. The weirdos.

"In our country too we have many who went crazy trying it," Natasha agreed. "Still, this really did seem to be how Buishenko could accrete—no: augment his support. We presume, naturally, he must have come on the secret by chance. Perhaps he located some alien-made thing which can protect him. Perhaps some scientist is working for him and has made a new discovery. At all costs we must find out. So we make plans to spy in his headquarters. That was formerly an emergency army base, underground in the Urals, intended for use in nuclear war. We have all the maps and can fix the alarms and booby-traps. But if we manage to steal this thing of his, what can we do with it? Soon no part of Russia—"

"We've heard all that!" Great broke in. "So what became of it? Is it at the bottom of the ocean?"

Natasha was incredulous for a moment. Then she threw back her head and pealed with laughter. "No, no! Our guess was wrong! It was not a machine that was so useful to Buishenko. It was a person. And though eight of our men were killed, we brought him safely away—Pitirim!"

There were long seconds of silence while they thought about the pasty-faced slack-jawed sickly boy. At last Jespersen said faintly, "Him? But what can he do?"

"Go into the alien city and return, bringing things with him," Natasha said patiently. "Which until now he has handed always to Buishenko. That man is a wild animal caring for no one but himself. I think—I hope—we are caring for everybody on Earth. Is it not better for Pitirim to give us what he can gather?"

VII

Crooning to himself, clutching his prize tightly in both dirty hands, Ichabod scurried crabwise along the dusty path, now and then chuckling and shaking back straw-fair hair from his bulging forehead. He paid no attention to the people coming and going around the shacks of scrap timber, plastic or salvaged bricks mortared with clay which he passed, and correspondingly they ignored him. Evernone knew Ichabod—a little touched in the head, but harmless, unlike some of the other kids.

The path wound randomly. He followed it as automatically as a trained rat in a maze. At one corner he stopped to relieve himself against a post, not letting go of what he held, and his crooning took on the words he had heard every Sunday, and sometimes weekdays as well, since he first learned to talk.

"Praise the Lord for He has sent
Angels from the firmament!"

(He knew exactly what the firmament was. It was a big town up near the stars. You couldn't go to it—though some people had impiously tried to—but you didn't have to. Not now.)

"Sinners He will likewise throw
To the raging fires below!"

(He knew what that would be like, too. His father had shown him by dropping his pet frog into the cookstove.)

Hardly waiting for the last drop to fall, he went on his way. When he came close to his home, though, he progressed more cautiously. It was one thing to have got hold of something which had belonged to the angels; it was another to keep it secret. If luck were with him, he might be able to slip indoors and hide it in his bed. He had to make it himself, so that was a good place to hide things. . . .

No. He couldn't sneak in. Peeking around the corner of the fence, he could see—and hear—his parents in the frame of the downstairs window. They were arguing as usual. Ichabod accepted such arguments as a fact of life. He would just have to wait until one or both of them went out.

Squatting against the fence, he wondered if he dared risk another glance at his treasure. Nobody was in sight. He opened his hands and gazed down with wonder and fascination. Surely this must be beryl, or chrysoprase, or—or one of the marvelous colored stones people said were used to build the palaces of heaven! Even between his hands it glowed red, green, blue, while if it were held up to the light it was dazzling!

"Hello, son. What have you got there?"

Gasping, Ichabod snatched the stone down between his legs, overcome by a wave of terror. He had been so absorbed he hadn't noticed the cat-footed approach of the man who had spoken. It wasn't anyone he knew, but a stranger—and he had been told that "stranger" almost beyond doubt also meant "sinner". He tried to huddle himself up so small that he would vanish from sight.

The man—he was medium-tall, but to Ichabod's frightened vision he seemed a giant—dropped on his hunkers and leaned forward cajolingly. "Show me what you got, son. It's pretty, isn't it?"

"You leave me alone!" Ichabod commanded fiercely.

The man rocked back, feeling in the pocket of his neat,

unmended jacket. "Show me, son. I might like to buy it off you. You ever had this much money, son?" He shook a dozen jingling coins in his outstretched hand.

"No! No! No!" Ichabod yelled, jumping to his feet and dashing up the noisy planking of the stoop before the house. The door swung open as he charged towards it, and he slammed full tilt into his mother's apron-front. Behind her he saw his father coming more slowly, his dark face set in a threatening frown which Ichabod for once found welcome.

"Make him go away!" he shouted.

His parents exchanged glances; then his father strode over to the stranger, who had risen to his feet and stood calmly on the path.

"A'right, mister—what've you been doing to my kid?"

"Nothing." The stranger smiled. Ichabod didn't trust people who smiled like that—just with their mouths. "My name's Corey Bennett. I do a little trading in rare artifacts. Do you have any idea what that thing your boy is holding might be worth in the right quarter?"

"What thing?" His mother glanced accusingly at Ichabod and shot out her arm. He tried desperately to cling to his treasure, but fingers like steel claws prised apart his grip and revealed the gorgeous polychrome glitter of the relic of angels.

"Ichabod!" she snapped. "Where did you snitch this?"

"I found it!" Ichabod wailed. "It's mine—give it here!" He stretched after it; a smart cuff above the ear was his reward, and he turned aside, blubbering, while his mother held him by the shoulder to stop him from running off. After a thoughtful examination of the flowing colors, she spoke up.

"Excuse my being uncivil, friend. I'm Martha Sims and this is my man Greg. You know what this thing is?"

"I reckon I will be able to, if I can take a closer look."

"Here then." She held it out. Bennett got up on the stoop and took it from her, studying it closely.

"Now wait a second!" Sims said. "That from the city?"

"Looks like," Bennett agreed.

"That's holy, then!" Sims stepped forward. "Martha, are you going to sell a holy thing to a sinner? It rightly belongs like all of its kind to—"

"You'd do well to talk less and work more, Greg Sims!" his wife broke in. "Can you eat it? Can you keep warm at night with it?"

"You sell that, you might as well sell your soul!" Sims raised his hand. "Bring the money-changers back to the temple, would you? I'll beat sense into you first!"

"Lay a finger on me and I'll lay a pole on you—I've done it before! At most I'll tithe it, but that's all, you hear?"

Bennett's shrewd dark eyes lifted for an instant from the gem, or whatever it was, and flickered over the faces of the couple. He gave a discreet cough and held the object out as though to return it.

"If it means something special to you, I wouldn't cause dissension," he said. "And the boy does seem to set store by it."

He was pleased to see the light of cupidity gleam now in Sims's eyes as well as his wife's.

"Got no business setting store by anything in this world," Sims growled. "Lay up your treasure in heaven—hear me, you little sinner?" He shook a fist towards his son, who cringed away. "Maybe the lesson he'll learn if it's taken—a lesson against avarice—maybe it'll outweigh the stain of passing it to an unbeliever."

"Who said I was?" Bennett objected. He made a quick pass with his hands; he had learned many such since arriving here and found them useful. "In my view this is what the relics are for. Don't we draw from them the funds which enable us to survive, an island of faith in a sea of unbelief? Doesn't the apostle say, 'To the pure all things are pure'? Money isn't evil in itself. Only lusting for it is."

Sims drew puzzled brows together. "Whose teaching do you follow, then?"

"Should it be anyone's but Brother Mark?" Bennett didn't wait for further comment, but rolled the gem around his palm; it was shaped like a long thin egg. "I don't know that this thing is *more* than pretty, though. . . . Well, someone should buy it gladly for a jewel. For the sake of feeding and clothing honest folk I'll take the chance. A hundred dollars."

He could see his pointed remark about lust for money had sunk deep in the minds of the Sims couple and was festering. Without making himself look dishonest, Sims couldn't argue the price up; his wife was only too well aware that if she tried to haggle her husband's piety might reassert itself and prevent any agreement. Ichabod had settled to a dull moaning.

While they were still hesitating, Bennett made it a hundred and twenty and closed the deal.

A genuine free trader—the notorious Den Radcliffe, for instance, or any of Grady's own buying staff—secure in the knowledge of a minimum thousand percent profit, might have paid twice as much and then had to bribe a federal agent as well before he could dispose of it as jewelery.

Corey Bennett *was* a Federal agent. And jewelery was the last purpose he had in mind for his prize.

He was almost light-headed with excitement as he picked his way out of the shanty town towards the highway. It was the second such settlement on this site. Refugees fleeing aimlessly from explosions at SAC bases south of here had established the first, but it had been burned almost at once by maddened troops after an abortive attack on the alien city. Some of the present inhabitants had lived through that, and—having nowhere else to go—had doggedly rebuilt. A much greater number were rootless wanderers, attracted to Grady's Ground because the rule of its self-appointed "governor" offered safety from federal law and a chance to get rich quick which had eluded them elsewhere, while another third or thereabouts were like the Sims family and had been lured by the widespread belief that the shining city was the home of angels sent to Earth to scourge sinners.

Bennett had learned to prove this latter view from the Book of Revelations. Practically anything, he had decided, could be proved from the same source.

Grady's Ground was in no sense an attractive place to live. The cities which had escaped destruction by maddened soldiers were overcrowded and dilapidated, while the shanty towns were still worse, and Bennett was relieved to be back on the highway where he had left his car.

But his heart sank when he saw a patrolman in one of the local peacock-gaudy uniforms standing beside the vehicle.

There was nothing for it but to walk up with an innocent expression. He did so, mopping his brow because the sun was strong today, while the dark glasses shielding the patrolman's eyes from the glare fixed him with the impassivity of a basilisk.

"Documents," the man said, one elbow on the car's roof, the other hand outstretched. Bennett produced them.

"Free trader," was the neutral comment. "O.K., what have you picked up today?"

In a split second Bennett made his decision. He was a comparative newcomer here, but already he had had a good number of "rare artifacts" pass through his hands—

or sacred relics, according to your point of view. He had dutifully paid on each the levy exacted by Grady's tax-collectors, who were more like a protection gang, in fact, though one had to admit that some of their take did get canceled into public services. It was unlikely that a lowly patrolman would risk offending him; his record suggested that one of these days he would bring off a really profitable coup.

So he dipped in his heavy pocket and displayed only a handful of the coins he carried because so many people around here had become disillusioned with paper money . . . not, including luckily, the Sims family.

"In that overgrown garbage pile?" he said. "Hell, those people won't trust anybody they haven't known for years. I thought I was coming to be pretty well respected, so I went and asked around, but clams aren't in the same class with them when it comes to keeping their mouths shut."

It was at least half true, and Bennett could see the patrolman's mind turning over. Inperceptibly he tensed, because if the man decided on a search he would have to risk jumping him. He had been hunting ever since his arrival for what he had obtained from Ichabod.

"O.K.," the patrolman decided, and handed back the documents. "Better luck next time. Show your face around more, is my advice. Make friends with one of their nutty religious groups. I could live the rest of my life on the stuff locked up in one of their tumbledown churches."

"Let me sell it on commission and you'll be able to afford two lifetimes instead of one," Bennett suggested, smiling. The patrolman cracked a faint grin in response and stood back.

It cost Bennett all his self-control not to touch the pocket where he had put the precious object, to reassure himself it was still there. But he managed it, and when he was well down the road found he had been holding his breath since starting the car.

Almost, he had recognized the thing when he saw it in the crippled boy's hand. The shape had seemed familiar, but the shining colors were so extraordinary he had thought he was confronted with some entirely new type of artifact.

This, though, was what he had been seeking. He had seen six or eight similar, all broken, all dull and colorless. This one was intact. He formed the words to himself: *in working order!* (Did that have a meaning? Did the aliens' products *do* anything, in the ordinary human sense?)

If that patrolman had guessed what I'm really up to. . . !

Piece by painfully gathered piece, the first complete alien "machine" to fall into man's possession was being assembled here under the very nose of Grady, to whom what he carried would be only a gewgaw for sale to some fat rich woman in Dallas or New York. The machine had cost two lives already, to Bennett's certain knowledge; once when a man tried to rob the store of a local church for a part rumored to match what he was looking for, once when Grady's patrols caught a man trying to smuggle something away for study at UCLA. Now, though, it was within sight of completion.

"And it's here in my pocket, the missing bit!" he whispered, trying to make the idea come real. "What's it doing? It's processing energy, that's for sure. What kind of energy? How much? *How?* Will I be able to tell without breaking it open and ruining it?"

And the worst question of all, of course, was this: what would the finished device do—this mysterious apparatus that he, third in line of succession, seemed fated to perfect? Like a three-dimensional jigsaw puzzle, it had been compiled from many sources. Suppose, after such effort, after such loss of life, it was something a human mind could never comprehend?

"Or something useless and pointless," he said to the air. "Like a bust of rich old Uncle Joe. But what the hell? We'll see. One of these days, we'll see."

He had been saying that to himself ever since the aliens arrived. It was becoming more and more difficult to believe.

VIII

It was as though humanity had fled in two directions through time from the catastrophe accompanying the appearance of the aliens. Or that was how it struck Orlando Potter, anyway.

Some small part had exploded towards the future, in the sense that many national boundaries had collapsed; here he was in Victoria, after all, on the southern tip of Vancouver Island, and nobody was raising objections because an American official was requisitioning Canadian facilities and had had his temporary office tied in by phone and teleprinter to the surviving nuclei of government in the United States. Of course rules, regulations and traditions had already taken a severe beating when the Canadian Parliament was transferred here in the immediate post-disaster period.

Curious, this preference for an island. A survival of British-oriented thinking, perhaps. Or possibly it was rather less subtle. Maybe they had simply foreseen the risk that the chaos now reigning on Grady's Ground might spread, wildfire fashion, and decided that Vancouver Island would be easier to hold against a wave of barbarism than a site on the mainland.

Because by far the majority of the human race had exploded towards the past, not the future. Remembering the civil wars in miniature that had been fought so bloodily south of here, especially in California, when panic-crazed city folk clashed with small-town vigilantes determined to keep what they had, Potter felt his mouth twist as though he had bitten a putrescent fruit.

That was a scattering backward through time, surely. To the days of closed peasant communities, suspicious of any stranger; worse, to the days of feudalism—for what after all was Grady but a feudal lord of the manor, governing his followers as absolutely as a medieval baron his serfs?

So now, ratlike, men squabbled and quarreled among the ruins of their once-proud civilization, and here and there a few of them toiled to assemble the broken pieces in a new form.

Can we coexist with the aliens? The question was an eternal one. *Can we simply draw back from where they have set their cities, and be our own masters everywhere else? After all, natural forces have barred us from parts of our planet in the past: deserts, icecaps, trackless forest. . . .*

Probably not. Potter wished achingly that the solution could be so simple, but he knew it would never happen. There were two insuperable obstacles: first, it was impossible to predict whether the aliens intended to spread further across the surface of the globe; second, it was not in keeping with the monkey-curious nature of man to ignore a mystery of this order.

He stared through the window of his temporary office, high in a recently built tower block. From it he could see the sea. The water was calm, and the summer sky was clear and blue. He would have preferred it storm-dark, to match his mood.

He was stuck here because of Pitirim. The original plan had been to fly him onward after their landing at Victoria, the nearest usable seaport; the whole of the far northwest of the USA was a fallout zone following the immense explosions at the ICBM sites there, and anti-missile missiles had created comparable havoc around all the conurbations further south.

But Zworykin had forbidden them to take the sick boy any further for the time being. The American and Canadian physicians and psychologists who had been flown to join him, under the leadership of the famous Dr. Louis Porpentine, concurred with his judgment. Life was being adequately, though precariously, maintained in his feeble body. His equally feeble mind, though, had suffered trauma upon trauma, what with being kidnapped from Buishenko's base under the Urals, and shot at by pursuit planes, and at last unceremoniously dumped in the Pacific. He was now terrified of his own shadow, literally, and it would be a long while before he could stand any further strain—even longer, perhaps, before he could be persuaded to cooperate with strangers the way he had obeyed Buishenko.

So: a temporary headquarters for "Operation Pantomime", as some idiot had code-named it—hence the use of terms like Harlequin and Columbine during the rendezvous at sea. It was his responsibility. He had pressed for its approval by the Committee on Emergency Countermeasures, and to go back without tangible proof either of success or of unavoidable failure was a prospect he dared not consider. His confidence was badly enough undermined already. So was the trust the rest of the committee reposed in him.

There were few surplus resources left here after the importation of Canada's emergency parliament. However, the facilities were tolerable. The standard of hospital care was as good as could still be found on the continent, and that was the chief consideration. There were the top four floors of this building, in near-new condition; moreover, the previous occupant had been an insurance company—

insurance was a bad line to be in during the post-disaster period—and had left behind a computer of very respectable capacity. The Canadian government had automatically requisitioned it, but they hadn't yet put it into service and were only moderately unwilling to let it go again. There were teleprinters and telephones, enough to go around, so Potter ought to feel he'd been very lucky.

In actual fact. . .

His head was beginning to ache from long staring at the bright sky. With an effort he brought his mind back to the tasks in hand, and took up the topmost of many sheets of paper from the in tray at his left. For a long moment he failed to make sense of it, and thought this was because his vision was swimming with after-images of the sunlit window. Then words penetrated—something about a policy on the life of a ship's captain—and he realized he was looking at the wrong side of it. Even in this country, formerly one of the greatest paper-producers in the world, it had become necessary to use both sides of the sheet. Some of the forests had burned for six weeks.

Turning the document over, he discovered the usual brief daily bulletin from the doctors attending Pitirim. It would have been summed up in three words: "Hardly any progress."

Heaven's name, how long is all this going to take? He thrust the paper blindly at the filing basket and took up the next report.

He was only halfway down the first of its ten paragraphs when he stiffened and began to read with absolute concentration—so total, indeed, that it was a shock when he came to the end and on glancing up discovered Greta facing him. He had not heard the door open. She was scowling.

"Yes?" he said—more abruptly than he had intended,

for his mind was still preoccupied with the implications of what he had just read.

"I think we're being made fools of," Great said. "Got a cigarette?"

"Oh—yes." Potter pushed an almost empty pack across the desk, and a book of matches. As she helped herself, he went on, "What was the point of that crack?"

"I said we're being made fools of," she repeated, dropping into a chair. "I don't believe for one moment that this idiot child they're fussing over is more than simply an idiot. I agree Buishenko may very well have stumbled across some way of getting in and out of the alien city, but mess the world is in, who turns out to have her bachelor's in science and says she decided to join the Scientific Service when she was fourteen—remarkable! Out on the boat that night when we made the rendezvous with the Russians I remember feeling very envious because along with all the rest it turned out you could string a few words of Russian together, while the best I can do is order a meal in Spanish. And then, the moment Natasha came aboard, you started to show another side of your character altogether."

She had become like ice now. He chipped at the frozen facade.

"Anything you can do. . . Isn't that about the size of it? She's a trained space-pilot; she's a first-rate engineer; she speaks marvelous English even though she's never been in an English-speaking country before. She overshadows you, and you took an instant dislike to her. Ever since you've been taking it out on me, on Abramovitch, on anybody who comes handy, and now you've decided to take it out on Pitirim as well."

"Give me one shred of proof," she said between her teeth, "and I'll write out what I said and eat the paper. Until you do, I'll go right on saying we've been made fools of, and you're behaving like the worst fool of all."

"Ever heard of weirdos?"

The question, as he had meant it to, surprised her. An answer struggled on the tip of her tongue with a continuation of her tirade, and emerged first.

"Hell, of course I have! What about them?"

"Define the term as you understand it."

"What is there to understand? You can't understand them. Supposedly they're people who tried to get into an alien city or spent too long trying to figure out an alien artefact and—well, something happened to them and they wound up filthy, hostile to ordinary people, and generally schizoid."

"Pitirim?"

Potter let the name hang on the air like a wisp of smoke. Greta did not stir to disturb it for long seconds.

At last she leaned to tap her cigarette-ash into a tray on the desk. With infinite weariness she said, "O.K., you win. Know what I was going on to say?"

He shook his head.

"I was going to talk some more about your parlor psychology. The way you manipulate people to serve your ends. But—oh, damn you. You're good at it. I never thought you'd pull it on me, but you just did, and it worked. Yes, yes, it can be argued that Pitirim didn't have enough of a mind to be driven crazy. . . . Oh, aren't you the clever son of a bitch, though? You're power-hungry—"

"No more than most people," Potter snapped. "If it hadn't been for the aliens, do you think I'd be deputy chairman of a congressional committee? The hell I would. I never wanted to be a Big Boss. I'd have had to pay too high a price."

"Maybe the talent came naturally, but you have it. You can make people feel weak and—and naked. You know how to lean on them, and when you feel like doing it you don't even pretend to be nice about it."

"Think weakness is a virtue?" Potter said harshly. "Do you? Garbage, it's a luxury! One we can't afford any more. We could get along when there was no competition bar other human beings, also with weaknesses like our own. But the aliens aren't people. If we're even going to survive in face of the challenge they present, we're going to know ourselves more intimately than ever before. We're going to have to criticize ourselves ruthlessly. We've got to give up making mistakes!"

Her only answer was a grimace. She stubbed her cigarette as though wishing she could crush him equally easily.

"But," he resumed, "as it happens none of this is of immediate consequence. Here, read this report, and then go pack your bags."

Hand poised to take the paper he was offering, she checked. "So you have decided to move me over!" she flared. "God, you're the most egotistical bastard I ever met! Nothing short of a space-pilot is good enough for you, is that it?"

Potter gave a weary sigh. "No. No, in fact in spite of there never having been much affection between us I shall miss you and hope you get back soon. I don't imagine you'll believe me, but I've never spent as long as ten minutes alone with Natasha and as far as I know she's shown no interest in me or any other man here. But we have to get someone reliable to Grady's Ground, right away. Since you complained when you came in about wasting time here on a fool's errand, I thought you'd welcome the assignment."

She had scanned the paper while he was talking. Now she said, not looking up, "I see. You're sending me there alone because there's a fair chance I may not come back. I'll no longer be a nuisance to you."

"Not alone," Potter said patiently. "Not if you can persuade one key man to cooperate. He can provide you with a flawless cover. Well?"

She pondered for a moment. Finally, sighing, she handed back the paper.

"Very well. This place is getting on my nerves. And so are you. It wouldn't be a bad idea for us to separate for a while."

"But the assignment!" Potter said. "Did you actually read all this?"

"Yes."

"Doesn't it—well, doesn't it sound. . . ?" He groped in the air as though in search of a word, and ended lamely: "Doesn't it sound exciting?"

"I don't think I know what that means any longer," Greta said, rising and turning to the door.

IX

It was abominably hot tonight. Restless, Waldron paced his apartment. For a while he tried to settle to his piano, but he felt oppressed and could not concentrate; all the channels on the TV were spewing forth infantile rubbish, repeats and old movies from the days before the aliens, and when he thumbed through his records not one item tempted him to set it on the player.

He stopped before the small table under the main window and for perhaps the thousandth time picked up what lay alone on the varnished wood. What *was* this damned thing? A stubby rod, eight and a quarter inches long, of something which was not glass but had cracked irregularly, glass-fashion, down the centerline, with spiny quasi-crystals embedded in its clear substance. From each apex of the crystal-like forms threads thinner than hairs wound out towards the surface—not in any formal pattern, but with a symmetry like that of a living organism.

A bit of garbage, tossed aside by a higher race. He had bought it nearly a year ago; it had cost him eight hundred bucks, and that was the lowest price paid at the auction sale he'd attended. Most of the other bidders had been speculators, as usual frantically seeking something from which a fortune might be made on resale to the government or to one of the corporations which still had research labs in operation. He had only wanted an object—any object—made by the aliens, as a barb for his mind.

Now, as occasionally before, the useless thing sparked his memory. Of course: he was neglecting the most important of his self-imposed tasks, the keeping of a journal which he had begun when he realized there was bitter truth in his habitual gibe about no one bothering to write history any more.

He picked up his recorder and carried it to his most comfortable chair. He poured a drink, then sat down and thumbed the control knob to recording position. He gave the date, hesitated, and suddenly uttered words he had not thought over.

"I have a mental picture of Washington. A pillar of smoke by day and a pillar of fog by night. A solid week now since Bennett walked into the City of Angels and died after Radcliffe's attack on him. Within hours of our reporting his suspected identity, they'd descended on us. I wasn't there because I'd had the night shift and was home trying to sleep. When I got back they'd sucked his body into the Washington fog and given strict orders not to mention the name Bennett to anyone. And a day later I received a call from somebody who wouldn't give his name, just a departmental reference—I traced it to the Secret Service—who commended me for not arresting Radcliffe and making it harder to hush this affair up.

"He didn't say 'hush it up.' But that was what he meant.

"Lord, I wish those underground bunkers in Washington hadn't been so efficient! The fires and the fallout might have cleaned house for us, and given new people with fresh ideas a chance to tackle our problems. Instead of which, we're stuck with pretty much the same old gang of hidebound bureaucrats and party wheeler-dealers, whose ideas fossilized in the Stone Age of the seventies. What's going to become of us with *them* still in charge?

"They must know that Bennett didn't walk in the front door of the City of Angels. That's been sworn to, over and over, and anyhow he wouldn't have been let in, looking such a mess—would he? So how did he get where they first spotted him? Did he materialize out of thin air? Did he jump clear from Grady's Ground, where Radcliffe said there are so many weirdos? Hell, it ought to have been the biggest news since—since the aliens landed!

"But I guess there's a protocol laid down. I guess it's 'not expedient' to investigate too closely. I guess it's all being smothered under labels saying 'Top Secret'. Maybe not even his brother has been told he's dead.

"If he has a brother."

He stopped abruptly. This was the point past which, ever since the chilling moment when Canfield brought him the news about the reversed identical prints, he had not dared to push his thinking.

A of M! The Age of Miracles is not past!

Into his moment of blankness the sound of the door buzzer broke like a sawblade. His hand flew to switch off the recorder. Who the hell could that be? He didn't want to be interrupted. Let the caller wear out his patience and go away.

But the caller had more patience than he'd expected. After the third buzz he leaned on the button and waited. Waldron jumped up with an oath and stormed to the door.

The sight of an elegantly dressed woman through the spyhole in the door brought an automatic assumption to his mind. Opening on a security chain, he said harshly, "I'm not interested! And watch who you pick on—there are still laws against prostitution and I'm in a position to enforce them!"

He made to slam the door.

"Lieutenant Waldron!" the woman snapped. She had colored a little, but betrayed no other reaction.

That shook him. If she knew his name and rank, clearly she was not just working her way around the bachelor apartments in search of a client for the night. Wondering, he unchained the door and swung it wide.

"I want to talk to you," the woman said. "About the death of Corey Bennett."

The words seemed to rest on the surface of his mind for a moment, as stones might rest on thin ice before breaking it. He looked her up and down. She was slender, almost as tall as he was; her face was rather thin, and jade-dust makeup lent her complexion a luminous pallor. Her fair hair was shoulder-long, gathered by a comb to the left so that it emphasized the delicate molding of her skull. She wore a dark-green bolero over rust-red leotards patterned with silver.

The ice cracked and the stones sank. He heard himself say, "*Corey* Bennett?"

The woman nodded, her expression sober. "I somehow expected that to surprise you. Here, you'll want to see my ID."

She zipped open a change-pocket on the hem of her bolero and proffered a small yellow card bearing her photograph. It identified her as Greta Helen Delarue, B.Sc., Office of the Federal Scientific Service, Washington D.C.

Waldron grunted. "Come to commend me for keeping my mouth shut?" he suggested sourly as he gave back the card. "O.K., come on in."

He waved her to the chair he had been using, picked up his drink, and sat on the edge of a table facing her. There was a brief silence. Eventually he had to make an impatient gesture. "So talk to me! You said you wanted to."

She was gazing at his alien artifact. "From the way you said '*Corey* Bennett?' I imagine you've already worked out a lot of what I thought I'd have to explain."

"I'm not allowed to talk about it to anybody," Waldron

snapped. "But I sure as hell have been thinking about it. I don't believe in identical twins with mirror-image prints."

"Correct. Corey Bennett was an only child. By the time our experts got at the body, organic death was well advanced—I must say your police surgeon isn't a paragon of efficiency, and that didn't help either—but we established his identity beyond doubt. And wound up with a far worse headache than before.

"Trying to figure out what turned him around?" Waldron said. "Well, what did happen to him?"

"I'll come to that in a moment." As soon as we—"

"What happened to him?" Waldron slammed his glass down on the table, and it rang into shivering fragments. He stared at the mess stupidly for as long as it took the pieces to stop rocking.

"I'm sorry," he muttered. "I'll get the disposall."

"Leave it, please! Why don't you sit down properly? I appreciate the strain you must have been under, but it'll make things a lot clearer if I can come to the point in my own way."

"Then get to it, instead of dancing all around it!" Waldron flung the words over his shoulder as he unhooked the disposall from its bracket and ran the nozzle over the wet table.

"Corey Bennett has been with the field branch of the Scientific Service since June last year," Greta said. "Four months ago he was assigned to a purchasing mission on what I gather you insist be called by the slang name of Grady's Ground. At present he is making good progress; his last report came in the small hours of yesterday morning."

"What?" The disposall thumped to the floor; Waldron kicked the power-switch before it could ingest the carpet, and spun to face her.

"I've been checking up on you, Mr. Waldron. Apparently you like to complain that nothing is being done about the—well, the aliens. I promise you, a great deal is being done. We simply dare not publicize the fact, though. For one thing, we'd face instant opposition from the re-lidges, and even though they're cranks there are a lot of them, too many for us to want to stir them up. For another, we're fairly certain that the aliens can read hostile intentions from a human mind. There's no other reasonable explanation for the way our armies were driven mad when they tried to attack their cities. The aliens could probably sterilize the planet if we annoyed them sufficiently, just as we could exterminate rats and mice if we sank all our efforts into the job. The most flattering assessment of their and our relative intelligence puts us no higher than rats.

"But we do what we can, and right now we have a problem which demands immediate and intensive investigation, but we have an incredibly small number of people to call on. Our resources are stretched so tight you can hear them twang.

"It goes like this. Corey Bennett is dead. His body is in one of our labs, being taken to very small pieces like a delicate machine. And Corey Bennett is at the same time probably engaged in the course of action which will lead to his death."

The following silence soughed through the room like a cold wind. In memory Waldron heard something which Maura Knight had said concerning weirdos. He moved to a chair, sweating.

"You mean he jumped through time as well as space to get to the City of Angels?" he said incredulously.

"It's the only halfway rational explanation we've hit on. Can you improve on it?"

Waldron shook his head feebly.

"Can't you—well, warn him he's in danger?"

"Do you think we dare?" Greta countered. "For all we

can tell, the warning might trigger the event. On the other hand, if we do nothing, we know that sooner or later . . . Oh, the poor bastard is a condemned man either way. All we can do is draw some profit from the situation. For the first time ever we're in a position to observe an alien process. It must be alien. And. . . Well, this is not supposed to be made known, but it's something you deserve to be told. Bennett's assignment was to try and complete an alien device which two predecessors had made progress with. According to his latest report, he thinks he now has all the parts, and he's going to assemble it and see what if anything it can do."

Waldron whistled. "Is it that which—which *twists* him?"

"That's what we're hoping to find out. Our theoreticians have suggested that he might have made a trip in Möbius space. Think of a hollow tube of triangular cross-section. Rotate one end through a hundred and twenty degrees and close it up into a ring. That would do it. Among the few things we know about the aliens is the fact that they're capable of intense local distortions of the continuum."

"Why are you telling me this? What does it have to do with me?"

"As much as you want it to."

"What do you charge for straight answers?" he snapped.

"I'm sorry. What first drew our attention to you, of course, was your fortunate decision not to arrest Radcliffe on a homicide count. I doubt if you did that for the right reasons, but it was a stroke of luck for us. That, plus the fact that apparently he attacked the girl he'd hired for the night and came close to being booked for assault on her, only you talked him round, left him with a debt of honor some time. Out on Grady's Ground, they tell me, they have the *omerta* bit in full form. And after the conclusion of your formal interview with him, we found something else on the tape—not very well recorded, but decipherable. He actually invited you to go out and join him on his home patch. Talking to his associate Hyson the following day, he specifically mentioned the offer again."

She raised her head and looked him square in the eyes.

"When you answered, your tone suggested that you found the proposition attractive."

Waldron felt perspiration creeping down his back. "That was then!" he barked. "I was angry at myself for something. I guess—" He hesitated. "I guess I'd invested Radcliffe, as a free trader, with a spurious artificial glamor. But I promise there's no risk of my throwing up my job and heading for Grady's Ground, even if he would like to hire me to run his security force."

"Very well, then." Greta started to her feet. "I'd hoped you might feel otherwise, but if I must I'll go on my own."

"Wait." Waldron felt a stab of puzzlement. "I—uh— I seem to have missed something, don't I?"

She approached the table by the window, letting her hand fall to the stubby cylinder which was not of glass. Shrugging, she said, "I've been assigned to watch Bennett do the things that will lead to his—arrival in the past. In my profession we aren't content to say 'A of M!' and forget about it. But on Grady's Ground it's difficult for an unattached woman to act independently. It occurred to us that if you were sincere in your complaints about the general apathy, you might be willing to exploit your contact with Radcliffe and provide me with a cover. It would make it a hell of a sight easier to get on the Ground, you know. They're fierce with strangers, and Radcliffe's safe-conduct would make all the difference."

There was a roaring in Waldron's ears. He felt as though the room were afloat on a rough sea. His stomach churned and his palms were wet.

Dear God! whispered some far-distant part of his mind. *It wasn't enough to talk about it. Something has to be done, sooner or later. And now I've got to be the one to do it. I didn't mean to get trapped, but I am trapped—I was never so frightened in my life and I don't want to say yes but if I don't how shall I ever be able to face myself again?*

His voice, however, was perfectly calm as he spoke. "Sit down again. Have a drink. I wish you'd mentioned this when you first came in. It would have saved a lot of time."

X

After Floodwood neither of them spoke for twenty hot miles; they sat, sweating and apathetic, while U.S. 2 went reeling under the wheels like an endless humming tape. Waldron had stopped at a drugstore in Duluth and bought a cheap pair of sunglasses, but they didn't completely screen the glare from the road, and wrinkling up his eyes made his forehead ache.

He had written to say he was arriving. But the U.S. mails did not recognize the existence of Grady's Ground, and there was no way to be sure the letter had reached Radcliffe. At all events there had been no answer. Still, they dared not wait forever.

The country, for some distance past, had begun to look neglected, like a room used but undusted for months on end. When there were people to be seen, they went timidly in patched shabby clothing. In every small town after Floodwood there were ruins burned by the mad armies— charred beams poked up from mounds of rubble, dark stains washed down by rain on the surviving walls, seedlings sprouting atop the mess.

But for the fact that the worst potholes in the road had been recently leveled with stone-chips and asphalt, Waldron would have taken it for granted that Minnesota had been abandoned by anyone with more ambition than to live as a grubby peasant.

A tilted sign stood by the road, its painted face chipped by bullets and cancerous rust eating at the metal: DANGER FALLOUT ZONE. From the anti-missile missiles around the Lakes, presumably; the wind would have carried a lot of the dust this way. But the count would have gone to safe long ago.

The people had fled from the fallout zone, of course—not officially evacuated, just panicking away. Where had they ended up? Shot on the Canadian border, maybe, or killed by disease, or trapped by despair in some refugee camp to the south—whatever had become of them, they hadn't returned. This area not only *looked* empty, which would have been a commonplace to a visitor from the crowded East; it *was* empty, and felt like an aboriginal wilderness.

Beside him Greta reached to the switch on the radio, and a sentimental pre-catastrophe ballad with a backing of lush strings oozed on the air. Waldron uttered a wordless objection: *Do we have to endure this garbage?*

"It's in character," Greta said. "We'll have to pass a border check somewhere soon."

"Already?" Waldron betrayed his astonishment.

She gave a twisted smile. "I thought you were the man with a map of Grady's Ground on his office wall."

"Stop needling me!" Waldron ordered savagely. Now the journey was nearing its end, all his half-formed fears were clamoring in the back of his mind again. *I thought my talk would never have to become action. . . .* He spoke aloud to silence the mental uproar.

"I was told that Grady controls North Dakota, part of South Dakota and Montana, a wedge of Manitoba, and only a narrow strip of Minnesota. Hell, we're not through Grand Rapids yet?"

"Not Grady's border post. Ours."

"What?"

"You never heard of such a thing. I know." She spoke with exaggerated weariness. "Christ, Jim, do you imagine the government wants to admit we've had to set up border posts on our own territory? They masquerade as forward defense posts, cordoning off the area dominated by the aliens. But they're border posts in fact if not in name, and it's no good claiming otherwise."

Waldron was at a loss for a moment. The sickly singing galled him. He said abruptly, "If you must play the radio to bolster your role, at least pick another station!"

The record ended. An unctuous voice said something about Lampo Products being better than.

"Can't," Greta said. "It's Grady's. Has a monopoly. Sabotaged every station for almost two hundred miles and trucked in all the gear he could to use for his own. Now it's the most powerful west of Chicago."

"Grady's? But. . . You mean he gets advertising?"

"Why not? There are a hell of a lot of people anxious to sell things to the richest community in North America."

"The richest?" Waldron felt like an idiot, parroting the succession of questions. He snapped his mouth shut, half-afraid of it hanging slack and foolish. Another pre-catastrophe record began, this time a pounding rock number.

"Jim, haven't you boned up on what you've let yourself in for?" Greta demanded. "I assumed you knew what it's like on Grady's Ground."

"I never had any intention of going there," Waldron sighed. "So what point would there have been in boning up? And least of all I never expected to go there to watch a man doomed to die and not tell him anything!"

"If only I'd realized," she muttered. "Better hurry with the questions. We can't have you pumping me for information once we're on the Ground. Somebody might start wondering how it is I know so much more than you do."

Waldron looked at her sidelong. No, she didn't give the

impression of being a well-informed person. Not any more. He couldn't determine what else the federal disguise experts had done besides coarsening the line of her mouth and rinsing her hair in some chemical to make it look bleached even though it was naturally fair. But the effect was unmistakable. Any man would assume that here was a selfish, pampered woman, losing her looks and afraid of it, but too spoiled not to be excessively fond of martinis, cigarettes and late nights.

She was supposed to be his mistress. It didn't say much for his taste or his sex appeal, in Waldron's view, but it was pointless to argue. This was the commonest type of woman now moving into the Ground—usually with a couple of failed marriages behind her—and so Greta Delarue had been transformed into Greta Smith, slut.

Putting up with her is going to be the worst part of the job. . . .

Aloud he said, "To start with, I want to know why you expect the border check so soon."

"There's a no-man's land. The border posts are on the line where the maddened troops were first affected. Some of them got closer before turning back, but none were initially affected further away. For a long while that was as far as they dared go. When they eventually tried to push ahead again, Grady was there and sinking roots. He likes having a big moat around his territory. It means he can run down smugglers without federal interference. He uses helicopters and Dobermanns."

Trying to recall the geography of the area, Waldron said, "Whose is Bemidji, then?"

"Nobody's. Or it would be if it was still there. It was razed during the madness. I've seen aerial photos. Nothing but rubble."

The announcer cut short the record and read another commercial. Greta turned down the volume.

"Jim, what kind of analogies do you have in mind for the situation on Grady's Ground? Or don't you have any?"

He was going to take a long time to get accustomed to her using his first name so—so *maritally*. He shrugged.

"I thought I had some ideas. You seem to be torpedoing them all."

"This is gold-rush territory. Grady has a monopoly on this continent of what's potentially the most valuable commodity in history, and he's sewed everything up tight. He runs the Ground on police-state lines, except that the major crimes aren't political—they're financial. Smuggling, for instance; failure to tithe alien artifacts, or pay a redemption fee in lieu. And so on. Everything is taxed, on top of being hideously expensive, and Grady is the chief tax-collector. Of course he does maintain the public services—the utilities which escaped the catastrophe, internal mail distribution, drainage and garbage clearance, the bare necessities. But do you know how much money he has to do it with?"

Waldron shook his head.

"The Revenue people calculate that the income from selling alien artifacts last year must have topped one and a half billion dollars."

She took a cigarette from her pocket and pressed the dash lighter home. "Grady, his staff, the top free traders, and a few others who've made themselves indispensable to the Governor, altogether about a thousand, are dripping money all over the Ground and hardly know what to spend it on. Like those oil-rich sheikhs used to out in the Persian Gulf. Gold-rush territory!"

The lighter popped out and she applied it to her cigarette.

"You'd think they'd try and close him out," Waldron said sourly. "Given that all alien artifacts are supposed to be federal property."

"How? By sending in another army and having it run wild all over the countryside the way the rest did? Lord knows how the aliens discriminate between an organized body of men and the riff-raff they tolerate on their very doorstep, but they manage it somehow. We have a hundred and thirty million people left to cope with. Grady's going to have to stew until we've put our own house in order."

And there it was: the border.

The road had been widened by the addition on either side of a large flat concrete pan. Concrete blockhouses with machinegun slits commanded the approaches and both pans, and barbed wire encircled the whole area, leaving only a gap on the road wide enough for a single vehicle and closed by heavy timber gates. In either direction stretched a line of watchtowers with searchlights and radar on top. An army helicopter was parked alongside the nearest blockhouse. Also there were six trucks: two of them heavily armored, the others—each with a trailer in tow—being two flatbacks and two tankers. They were painted dull gray.

"That's a bit of luck," Greta said softly, turning up the radio a little. "An ingoing convoy."

"So I gather. Why a convoy?" Waldron took his foot off the accelerator and let the car coast towards the gates.

"The no-man's-land is rugged and full of lakes; a lot of hijackers work it, so the wealthiest residents on the Ground bring in their household supplies under escort. And goods for other people too, of course—at a price."

A voice boomed from a loudhailer, ordering them to halt. As soon as the car stopped, a sergeant and two privates, all with slung carbines, appeared to open up for them and waved them towards a clear spot on the nearer pan. The sergeant approached with a bored expression.

"Read this and signify that you understand it," he told Waldron, proffering a much-stained printed form pasted on a card. Waldron scanned it: now entering a zone defined as an emergency zone by Federal Emergency Regulation nomber so-and-so, act of proceeding beyond this point implies recognition that the Government of the United States cannot be held responsible for—et cetera. *A polite way of saying you're going abroad,* Waldron translated.

He returned the card. The sergeant beckoned the nearer private, who took out a notebook and scribbled down the license number of the car before coming to ask their names.

"O.K., wait there," he said. "May take a while."

Greta put on a sour expression. "We have to sit out here scorching to death? What for?"

The private gave her a grin full of stained teeth. "For all I know, lady, you and your pal murdered grandma and pawned the family jewels, hm? Or maybe it's a hot car and I don't mean from the sun." He grinned again and went into the blockhouse. The sergeant had walked over to the tail truck of the convoy and was talking to a man leaning down from the armor-glass window of the cab. The remaining private stood staring at Greta with his gun leveled and his jaws chomping rhythmically on a wad of gum.

Waldron's hand went to his pocket and began mechanically to stroke his alien artifact, which he had picked up just before setting out. *As an amulet? Have we become that irrational?*

Time passed. From the blockhouse emerged two men in sweat-damp overalls, guns belted at their waists; one of them was stuffing a packet of papers into a satchel. They must have been going through some form of clearance procedure, Waldron decided. The first to catch sight of Greta nudged his companion and rounded his lips in a mocking whistle. They both advanced on the car.

"Waiting got you down, sugar?" the first man said, bending to the passenger's window. "Why don't you ditch this creep and ride along with us? We're pulling out right now."

"Yeah," the other supplied. "You stick with this guy, you could be here all day. I bet they're going through every wanted file they got looking for his ugly pan—hey, Rick?"

Chuckling, Rick glanced at Waldron for the first time. A startled expression crossed his face. He said, "Just a moment, Bill. Mister, is—is your name Waldron by any chance?"

Waldron stiffened. Yes, it is. How the hell did you know?"

"Jesus!" Rick straightened. "Bill, get in there and tell that assheaded soldier to quit messing around and clear this car to ride in with the convoy. This here is our new security chief. The boss said he'd be arriving soon!"

Waldron and Greta exchanged looks of astonishment. In an agony of apology, Rick mumbled excuses for not having recognized them, and Waldron dismissed them with half his mind while the other half wondered why in the world Radcliffe had not replied to his letter, given that he had obviously received it.

Well, it wouldn't be long before he had a chance to ask in person. Here was Bill coming back, and the private looking horribly embarrassed, and the sergeant bawling him out, and one way and another it was clear that around here Den Radcliffe swung rather more weight than the Army and the federal government put together.

XI

Den Radcliffe sat under an awning on the upper-level balcony of his house. He had had it built for him by an architect who was almost pathetically grateful. Since the catastrophe he had designed nothing but emergency prefabricated apartments to be stacked on top of one another like drawers in a chest. Radcliffe's assignment was so perfect an opportunity to pretend that the world was back to normal, he would probably have accepted it without pay.

There were eighty-eight rooms. There was a private lake. There were fortifications on nearby hilltops. There was an underground generating plant which could be switched from diesel to windmill or watermill drive if need be, diesel fuel being imported and expensive. The building was the modern counterpart of a medieval baron's castle, capable of withstanding siege . . . if not nuclear attack.

But one didn't have to worry about that any more.

Gradyville was just out of sight behind a row of hills. So was the alien city. When there was low cloud, the light from the latter could be seen reflected in the sky. That was the one thing Radcliffe regretted about the site he had chosen for his home.

A phone buzzer sounded. He said to the air, "Get that!" While someone got it he went on wondering whether he should go down to the lake for a swim or merely call for another beer.

He was feeling very pleased with himself. He had put over on Grady the slickest piece of trickery anyone had ever managed against the big greedy slob. He had come back from his recent trip around the States to be greeted by his apologetic staff with bad news. The greater part of a convoy of goods he had dispatched from California had been hijacked in no-man's-land. The total value of the lost consignment was about a hundred thousand dollars, on which he would have stood to pay Grady fifty percent import duty.

He had stormed and reprimanded left and right; he had fired his security chief—Waldron's letter had arrived during his absence, and offered a providential bonus for the scheme; in sum he had generated an impenetrable smoke-screen. Behind it he had quietly sold off the goods under Grady's very nose, making a handsome profit *and* escaping the duty. The hijackers had been a team of his own men—not his estate staff, but members of his private army about which Grady knew only that it existed.

Radcliffe had built up that army by slow, cautious degrees. It came in handy for operations like mock robberies, but that was not its real purpose. Ultimately it was destined to oust Grady and install Den Radcliffe as his successor.

He chuckled, picturing the look on Grady's face when he learned he was about to be deposed.

"It's Rick Chandler," the girl who had taken the phone-call reported. "The convoy is just leaving the Ball Club post now. They're bringing in the new security chief, too."

Radcliffe gave a satisfied nod. On this convoy, of course, he would meekly have to pay the duty, but to have sneaked even one load through without—

"What was that?" His head snapped around. The girl, dark-haired and quite naked, stood in the opening of the double glass doors leading on to the balcony, clutching the

114

phone. He liked to have naked girls around him. "Did you say the new security chief?"

"Mr.—uh—" A frown creased the girl's tanned forehead; she found remembering things rather difficult. "I guess he did say what the name was, but I forgot it again." Her voice was flat, characterless, like a machine's.

"Give me the phone!" Radcliffe barked.

Frightened, the girl came running, almost tripping over the extension cord. Radcliffe cursed her for a clumsy idiot, and she dropped the instrument at his side and fled.

"Rick!" he exclaimed. "Is it right that you got Waldron with you?"

"Sure we do. I—uh—I guess I have to admit I didn't recognize him straight off, but you showed that picture and I thought he looked kind of familiar, so I up and asked him, and it's him O.K. I've seen his ID. He's the one."

"When you get here, bring him straight to see me," Radcliffe ordered.

"Yessir. And his girlfriend too?"

"He's not alone?"

"No, he has this blonde along. Dye-and-paint job and not so young as she once was."

"Hmm!" Radcliffe pondered. "Get one of your men to take over his car, then, and have Waldron and the woman to ride with you in the lead truck. Talk to him, get acquainted. I want your opinion of him, and some of the other men's, before I definitely hire him. The starch doesn't wash out of a cop that easily, you know. If he's not the type you can get along with, I'll have to go look for someone else."

"O.K., Mr. Radcliffe," Rick said. And added after a pause: "It's good thinking, sir. I know some of the guys aren't too happy about the idea. But me, I trust your judgment and I'll do my best to talk 'em around."

Radcliffe set the phone down, very thoughtful. Waldron's letter had seemed like pennies from heaven when he found he could tie it in to the pattern of deception he'd woven to bolster the mock hijacking. Over the past few days, however, he'd been having second thoughts, which was why he had not written back extending a formal invitation, and he had been winding up to telling his men that there had been a change of plan.

Still, here he was, and it might turn out for the best in the end. He called philosophically for another beer and went on musing.

It was phrased as a polite request; nonetheless it was an order, and Waldron complied, letting Bill take over his car while he and Greta accompanied Rick to the armored monster heading the seven-vehicle string. He was curious to know what the armor was protecting apart from the occupants, and when he saw crates of liquor and exotic foods he was mildly amused . . . and more so when he heard the tankers contained gin.

It was convenient to have this post of authority ready-made for him. He could reasonably inquire about details of Radcliffe's organization which no ordinary stranger would be told. Moreover if they had driven in alone they might have run foul of hijackers or had to bribe Grady's patrols even for directions to get where they were going.

There were comfortable padded seats in the back of the cab, plenty large enough for Rick, Greta and himself. He passed cigarettes, learning as he did so that the driver was called Tony.

"I—uh—I heard about you from Mr. Radcliffe," Rick ventured. "You did him a good turn when he was in the East, that right?"

"More sort of prevented him doing himself a bad one,"

Waldron answered dryly. "Say, how did you come to recognize me, anyhow?"

"Oh, Mr. Radcliffe showed us your letter, and he had this photo of you from somewhere. Don't know if you sent it—did you?"

Waldron shook his head, impressed with Radcliffe's efficiency but a trifle disturbed also.

"Pretty good likeness, too," Rick went on. "Of course I should have looked at you before I . . . What is it, Tony?" In response to a muttered exclamation from the driver.

"Only a weirdo," Tony answered. "Thought for a moment it was someone else."

"A weirdo? Where?" Greta had spoken little since leaving the border post; now she craned around like a tourist.

"Over there." Rick pointed through the side-window of the cab. "Like a scarecrow—see him?"

Some thirty yards off the road, on a hillside thick with weeds, a man was standing stiff as a post, his clothes ragged, his face turned ecstatically to the sun and his eyes wide.

"What's he doing that for?" Greta whispered. "Looking at the sun like that, he'll go blind!"

"Maybe that's what he wants," Rick said contemptuously. "How can you figure what goes on in a weirdo's head? Nutty as a candybar, him. Tony, why are you so nervous?"

"I thought for a moment he might not be a real weirdo," Tony muttered. "That's how the boss lost that big load the other day, right? Guy spotted the convoy by making like a weirdo, gave the signal for the hijackers."

"Mr. Radcliffe had something hijacked?" Waldron probed.

"Afraid so," Rick confirmed, and told the story. He, naturally, accepted that the robbery had been genuine; Radcliffe had carefully restricted the number in the know.

"Is that going to be one of my jobs here?" Waldron said. "Preventing hijackings, I mean?"

Rick nodded. "The guy before you didn't do so well," he said. "That's why the job came vacant." He hesitated. "I guess I ought to say," he concluded, "that it'll be vacant again if it happens twice."

"Oh, I didn't come all this way to turn around and go straight home," Waldron answered with a confidence he did not feel. Out here, away from the familiar surroundings and the pretended normality of New York, he felt naked and terribly vulnerable. But he must put a good face on things at all costs.

A few miles further on, Tony began to whistle under his breath. Glancing up, Waldron realized why. They had traversed the no-man's-land. While the U.S. government might prefer to call its border posts anything but, Grady had no such scruples. Ahead was a squat concrete building on whose roof an enormous garish red-and-white sign announced **GRADY'S GROUND!** complete with exclamation point.

"Two miles to Gradyboro," Rick said contentedly. "Then just another twenty or so to Gradyville, and a mile and a half beyond and there we are." He peered past Tony's shoulder. "Who's coming out for us—can you see?"

"Mother Hubbard," Tony grunted.

"Ah, shit. Just our luck."

Guards in musical-comedy uniforms barred the roadway; at their head was a bulky woman with gray hair cut man-short who alone among the dozen or so carried no gun. Tony wound down the window beside him and leaned out.

"Evening, Captain Hubbard!"

The woman didn't return the greeting. Her face was as

sour as a green apple. "What you got this trip?" she demanded. "Where you been?"

"General purchasing mission. Over around the Lakes."

"Ah-huh. Want to pay up now or have everything listed and sealed?"

"Better seal it, I guess. It'll be quicker. We have an important passenger along." Rick gestured for Waldron to show himself, and Tony presented him. "Ex-Lieutenant Jim Waldron of the New York police, our new security chief."

"Started well, hasn't he?" Captain Hubbard grunted.

"What?"

"Kept the hijackers off you this trip, I mean." She turned away, signalling to her subordinates, who promptly and efficiently began to inspect the contents of all the trucks.

"I wasn't expecting this," Greta ventured. "It all looks so—well, so *official.*"

Rick gave a proud-father smile. "We're no messy barbarian mudhole here," he said. "They tell me this is the richest community in North America—did you hear that?"

A fragment of history was chasing around Waldron's skull. Abruptly he caught up with it. "Katanga," he murmured.

"What?" Rick said, on the verge of leaving the cab.

"Nothing." But Waldron saw that Greta had reacted to the word and was nodding.

It took only half an hour or so to list and seal their cargo, and then they rolled again. Darkness was gathering as they reached Gradyboro, and huge neons were lighting the façades of the few intact buildings, advertising in about equal proportions gambling and girls. There were no streetlamps, but their absence didn't matter. On several streetcorners they saw groups of people waving banners and handing out tracts to passers-by.

"Relidges," Rick explained in answer to a question from Greta. "Cranks who think there are angels in the alien city. We put up with them. They do our dirty work for us. Not bright enough to do more than haul garbage, most of 'em."

It was fully dark by the time they reached Gradyville, equally bright, a gap-toothed city where ruined buildings had been cleared and the rubble leveled and tents and trailer-homes had moved into the vacant sites. By then Waldron was so tired, he found he could not remember the original names of these towns which Grady had renamed after himself. There was also a Gradywood further on.

"That's the governor's place," Rick said, gesturing at a distant floodlit edifice with fountains playing before its portico. "Big—but wait till you see ours. Grady just took that one over and dolled it up. Mr. Radcliffe had his built special."

The convoy, headlights ablaze, rounded the shore of a darkling lake, and there it was: Radcliffe's mansion, a sprawl of armor-glass and reinforced concrete faced with colorful tiles, with pools and flowerbeds and a horde of scurrying servants who closed in on the trucks, and a scatter of lesser buildings all around, some looking like defense posts, others like barracks or family accommodation.

"I'm to take you straight to Mr. Radcliffe," Rick said, helping Waldron and Greta down from the cab. "And when he says straight, he means it. Sorry. I guess if you need to go to the can we could spare that much time, but that's the limit."

So, barely having had time to glance around, they were escorted into the house, along a corridor with one glass wall fronting the lake, through a door and into a room dominated by a vast dining-table at the left end of which sat Radcliffe in an immaculate white suit, contemplating the remains of what must have been a gourmet's dinner. But at the other end of the table . . .

Waldron's heart lurched in his chest.

"Ah, Mr. Waldron!" Radcliffe said silkily. "I see you recognize my companion. Well, I told you I'd get what I paid for, didn't I? One way or another!"

He gestured for Rick to leave the room. Waldron didn't notice his departure. His eyes were riveted on the woman —not on her body, though she was completely naked, but on her face. It was a vacant face now, almost devoid of intelligence, but there was no mistaking the identity of Maura Knight.

XII

A long and terrible silence followed as empty of time as of sound. Waldron had no idea whether it lasted seconds or minutes. Eventually Radcliffe stirred.

"Thank you, Maura. You may leave us now. Have someone come with drinks for Mr. Waldron and his friend."

Obedient as a trained dog, Maura rose from her chair. As she passed Waldron on the way to the door, her eyes scanned his face, and briefly a gleam of recognition shone in them; then she was gone, and he was reacting with a fit of almost physical nausea.

"Sit down," Radcliffe invited, waving at chairs on his right. "Ah . . . I didn't have to introduce you to my girl-friend, but I don't believe I've met yours." He cocked a sardonic eyebrow.

Mechanically Waldron shaped words. "Greta—Greta Smith. We—uh—we decided to travel together. I hope you don't mind."

"Mind? Hell, no. Sensible of you. Half the women on the Ground are whores and the rest are so damned ugly you wouldn't want to look at them twice. Apart from those who are in service with free traders, I mean. We can get the best in that area, too. Heh-heh!" He chuckled thickly, and Waldron realized abruptly he was drunk. He carried his liquor well, but the tell-tale signs were perceptible in his voice and his flushed face. "Come on, sit down —how often do I have to tell you?"

They complied. Radcliffe leaned both elbows on the table and stared fixedly at Waldron.

"Well! What made your mind up for you, then? I'd more or less decided you were too fond of your roots to do more than talk about coming here. It was kind of a surprise when I got your letter."

Waldron had to lick his lips. The shock of finding Maura here had reminded him with painful vividness of the night of their first meeting, and though he could only guess what Radcliffe had done to get what he had paid for he could be damned sure it wasn't pleasant. "I got tired of making phony gestures in a smelly office, like you said I would. I wanted to see if it's true that out here things actually happen."

"Has meeting Maura again changed your mind back where it was?"

Waldron hid his hands under the table so that he could drive the nails into the palms unobserved. He said, "I didn't think she was likely to speak another civil word to you. What did you do?"

"None of your business," Radcliffe said, and laughed. It was a horrible laugh, half drunken, half mocking. "Are you shocked, Waldron? If so there's no point in your staying here. Except maybe you could gang up with a bunch of relidges. We don't live by the book here, you know. We don't waste our time filling out forms and inventing petty regulations. I guess it'll take you a while to get used to that. Maybe you'll never make it. Some people don't."

A liveried manservant tapped at the door and brought bottles and glasses on a trolley. Radcliffe held out his own glass with an imperious gesture and before serving the guests the man half-filled it with straight whisky.

"Coming in with Rick's convoy," Radcliffe went on,

"you must have got better acquainted with Grady's Ground than most newcomers manage right away. What do you think of it? Is it like you expected?"

"I wasn't sure what to expect," Waldron parried. He wanted very much to look at Greta, maybe draw her into the conversation, but he dared not. Her role was exclusively that of a sexual convenience he'd brought along; as much attention as possible must be diverted from her if she were to have any hope of carrying out her mission.

"The hell with that," Radcliffe said. "I'll tell you what you were expecting, shall I? I've seen enough strangers react like you. You expected a kind of Wild West show, a patch of anarchy, an every-man-for-himself sort of scene. Balls! We have the civilized amenities. We got flush toilets. We keep our roads mended. We pay taxes, for Chrissake." He chortled as though at a private joke. The sound turned into a burp. "We got patrolmen—like regular police except a lot of people who came here thought that was a dirty word. We run this like a modern country, with radio, TV, phones, everything. What's more they work. Yes, that's what it looks like: a modern country. But do you know what it *is?*"

He was leaning so far forward now his chest was almost touching the polished tabletop, and his voice was gruff with the intensity of sudden emotion. Greta, alarmed, fumbled for Waldron's fingers under the table.

"I said do you know what this place is? It's a rathole! It's not a country or a community or an empire or what the hell label they last stuck on it! It's a nest of *god damned rats.*" He spaced the words with emphatic care.

"Know something, Waldron? Last time I saw you I was out of the hole. I was on human territory. I was kidding myself I was still a man, rational, intelligent, master of our own planet. And when they radioed me you'd shown up, I got to thinking. I been drinking with it. You noticed." He drained his glass and threw it tinkling to the floor.

"That kid Maura . . . A rat! Hear me? That's all any of us are—rats, and worth no more than rats. You think I oughtn't to have changed her mind to get what I paid for? You think she didn't deserve it? You do, damn you! I can see it in your eyes!" Radcliffe slapped the table with his open palm and leaped to his feet so violently he overset his chair.

"Hell, then! I'll have to prove I'm right! I won't have you sitting there thinking you're really a man!"

He stormed to the door and bellowed at the top of his voice for Rick Chandler. Waldron, not moving, remembered that infinitely long ago he had sat in his office and compared free traders like Radcliffe to the same animals: rats, preying on the work of a higher species.

The two identical cars which were waiting at the door when Radcliffe harshly ordered them out of the house were familiar to Waldron only from pictures: silent, luxurious Mercedes limousines with recirculating Freon-vapor engines listed at a basic price of forty-thousand dollars and supplied before the advent of the aliens to heads of state and royalty-in-exile only. Rick, looking very tired and struggling to hide his ill temper, was at the wheel of the one into which they followed Radcliffe; the driver of the second was accompanied by four armed bodyguards, two black and two white.

"Take 'em up and show 'em the aliens!" Radcliffe barked, and slumped against the cusions.

Greta gave a whimper of alarm. Waldron wondered how much of it was genuine, how much feigned. He himself was very frightened. The dark night seemed full of unspeakable menace, and Radcliffe, drunk and depressed, was in a dangerous mood. But there was nothing he could do except keep quiet in the hope of not making his new employer still more angry.

The road they took led past two shanty towns where there were no lights but kerosene lamps, dim in unglassed windows, and another small town almost as shabby, almost as dismal, emitting a stench of sewage that percolated the car's airconditioning.

"Rats!" Radcliffe repeated, sniffing and jerking his thumb at the car's window.

Waldron tried to orient himself, but failed. He had covered up the roads and names on this part of his map with the lopsided five-pointed star of silver foil he'd pasted to it. He had made it far larger than scale, thinking otherwise it would not show up well enough. And indeed its glow must cover a huge area; the highest hill ahead was peaked with a roseate aura.

Moving towards him as though for protection, Greta asked diffidently, "How—how much further?"

"We can get a clear sight from the next rise," Rick answered. Radcliffe snapped at him.

"Don't stop there! Keep right on going until I tell you!"

Rick gulped audibly, and then nothing more was said for long minutes.

They could see it.

Monstrous beyond conceiving, as though the cities of London and Tokyo and New York had been piled together and turned into a translucent, mist-veiled, iridescent unity. The natural features of the landscape had been ignored; somewhere under the shining mass there had been lakes and hills, roads and small towns, woods and fields— and they *were not,* stamped flat like lumps in muddy dirt. Stabbing hundreds of feet into the night, shafts of luminescence rose: a myriad gems thinned to the substance of a higher cosmic plane. Lights sharp as stars flashed and faded, and the colors rioted—tonight, the commonest was rose-pink, but ever and again blues, greens, pure flame-yellow and white of a clarity to terrify an onlooker crossed the background and dissolved.

Opal and chalcedony, jade and chrysolite, jacynth and amber, ruby and emerald, everything which mankind had ever meant by the word "jewel" was epitomized in this majestic, awful creation: sixty-six miles from the tip to the furthest tip of its deformed pentangular outline. Waldron's mouth was dry. He wanted to shrink away from his eyes, cut the nerves conveying knowledge of such a reality to his brain. Not only the sheer integrated size of the alien city—for from this point one could see a mere fraction of it—but the implication that its builders must be not simply more powerful, not simply more advanced than man, but utterly and inconceivably different, made him cringe and whimper silently: *I dared imagine we could act against them? I was a stupid arrogant fool.*

"We live off their garbage," Radcliffe said in a thin voice. "How do they think of us? The way we think of flies and maggots. . . ? Rick, stop the car."

Face beaded with sweat, the driver obeyed. The lights of the second car bloomed briefly in the rearview mirror as it swung out and came to a halt alongside.

"How—how is it obtained?" Waldron forced out. "I mean the garbage."

"Oh, it turns up all over the countryside for about fifty miles in any direction," Radcliffe sighed. "As though they throw it away at random when they have no further use for it. I—" He hesitated, uncharacteristically, as though the awe-inspiring vision before them had sobered him. "I keep a bit which killed a kid," he concluded. "Came slamming in through the window of his room. Cracked his skull."

"You—uh—you keep a watch on the place?" Waldron hazarded. "Try and spot the stuff as it comes out?"

"Oh, sure, we tried that. Or rather Grady did. Can't be done. You can't see it being tossed out, you can't photograph it, you can't pick it up on radar. . . . I guess it kind of skips the first bit of its trip."

Greta's hand closed painfully on Waldron's arm. He knew why she had reacted so violently. Corey Bennett, too, had "skipped."

Or rather: he's going to.

"So we gave up," Radcliffe said. "Only people now who keep watch on the city are relidges. Some of them out there tonight, in fact. Hear them singing?"

Until this moment Waldron hadn't noticed the sound; when his attention was drawn to it, he found he could hear it clearly, slow and solemn and rather sweet.

"Show 'em, Rick," Radcliffe ordered. Rick switched on a powerful spotlight attached to the side of the car's windshield and swiveled it around. Its beam sworded across a small group of ragged men and women, a few hundred yards distant on a bare hillside, staring with adoration at the alien city.

"You saw some like that back in Gradyboro, remember?" Rick said to Waldron and Greta. "They come out here one or two nights a week and sing hymns through to dawn. Bring their kids and all. In the rain, too. Even in the snow I've seen 'em."

For the first time Waldron felt less than contemptuous of the fanatics who had jumped to the conclusion the aliens were visitors from heaven. Certainly they must be closer to the angels than mankind. . . .

"Rick, douse the light!" Radcliffe had glanced to his left; now he was peering down the dark hillside. There a dry gully was shielded from the otherwise all-pervading luminance of the city, and something like a firefly was moving across it, flickering irregularly a few feet from the ground.

"Someone carrying a flashlight?" Rick suggested.

"Flashlight hell!" All the drunkenness and maudlin depression had vanished from Radcliffe's tone. "Look, it's changing color all the time. Call the other car. I want whoever it is surrounded—quick!" He flung open the door.

Rick uttered brief commands to a radiophone under the dash, and the guards leaped from the second car and spread down the hill towards the darting polychrome gleam.

"What is it?" Greta asked.

"Could just be that someone's found a live relic," Rick grunted. He fumbled out a cigarette and lit it without taking his eyes from the half-seen men fanning out around the spark of light. It had stopped moving, as though its bearer had realized he'd been spotted and was minded to turn tail.

"A live relic?" Waldron echoed.

"Mm-hm. Turned on, or whatever. In working order, I guess you'd say. I've seen a few, but they're pretty rare. The boss got thirty thousand for a big one last summer. He won't let this one slip through his fingers, that's for sure."

XIII

Ichabod's first horrified thought as the moving shapes closed on him out of darkness was that his impiety in coveting the pretty relics of the angels had worn out their patience, and avengers were coming to punish him for his sins. Then a flashlight beam sprang up, and he realized those approaching were merely men. Not that that was any great comfort. They would certainly take his prize away from him. Like that nasty Mr. Bennett!

Silent tears coursing down his cheeks, he stood with his treasure englobed in both hands, its brilliant multicolored splendor leaking out between his fingers. If he had thought of stuffing it inside his shirt . . . But it was too late now.

He cast a frantic glance towards the spot, higher on the hill, where his parents sang lustily with their friends under the fervent exhortation of Brother Mark, and wished he could turn back time and once more find himself on the fringe of the group, cancel his decision to sneak off and search for another beautiful heavenly jewel to replace the one his parents had sold.

"Why, he's only a kid," one of the silhouetted men said to another.

"And crippled with it," confirmed the second man. "Hey, is the boss around? Didn't I see him get out of the front car?"

"I'm here!" an authoritative voice called from slightly

135

higher up the hill, and the speaker came scrambling and grunting to Ichabod's side. "Get it away from him, Gabe."

Reflexively Ichabod tucked his hands, and the thing he held, between his legs and doubled up, yelling. It was no good. Strong fingers pried loose his grip and held up the coruscating ball.

There were low whistles, and by the ball's light faces could be seen reflecting awe. "That's a beauty!" one of the men said in an impressed tone. "Never saw one that bright before."

"Give it here," Radcliffe said, and it was placed in his palm. It was about three inches in diameter, slightly warm, slightly slippery from Ichabod's perspiring clutch; that apart, it was ordinary to the touch, being about as smooth as window-glass. Its appearance, though, was not at all ordinary. Within its translucent depths moved colors as rich and varied as those of the city itself. Radcliffe's earlier despondent mood had faded the moment he saw this object in the distance; now he felt it return, but tinged this time with gentle envy of beings who could create such lovely things.

"Why should they want to chuck away something like that?" Gabe asked rhetorically.

"By mistake?" offered another of the guards.

"You really think *they* can make mistakes?" Gabe countered, and that question went unanswered.

Radcliffe turned to the soundlessly weeping Ichabod with an ingratiating smile. "Where did you find this, son?" he cajoled. "Right near here, was it?"

"None of your business!" Ichabod retorted.

"Oh, come now, son," Radcliffe reproved. "Sure, it was very smart of you to find it, but finding it doesn't make it yours, you know. Didn't your mom ever tell you that when you find something you got to give it back to . . . ?"

"Boss!" Sharply from Gabe. "Trouble's coming!"

Radcliffe swung around. The relidges had ceased their singing, and a group of half a dozen had detached themselves and were heading this way in the wake of a tall man with a full black beard, wearing a black robe with a big silver cross hung around his neck on a thong.

"Gabe, go back to the car and ask Rick for all the cash he has on him," Radcliffe instructed. "For a relic like this they'll probably stand out for at least a thousand."

"Boss, I have a thousand right in my pocket," Gabe grunted. "But don't you know who that is leading them? That's Brother Mark. You could offer him a million and he'd only curse you for a wicked sinner."

"So that's the famous Brother Mark, is it? How do you know? I've never seen him, or even a picture of him."

"Right. He says photos are graven images, and forbidden. But my kid sister is in his church." Gabe spat sidelong by way of comment on his sister's views.

They waited. The relidges advanced at a steady pace, not hesitating or hurrying even when they came close enough to see that Radcliffe's men carried guns. Ichabod let out a wordless yell when they were ten paces off, and hobbled at maximum speed to throw his arms around the man third from the front.

"What the hell . . . ? I mean what are you doing here?" the man gasped. "Brother Mark! It's my boy Ichabod!"

Brother Mark took no notice. He marched straight up to Radcliffe and held out his hand.

"Give it to me," he said. "It's holy."

Radcliffe studied him. He was an impressive figure: very tall, high-browed, with deep-set dark eyes. But Radcliffe was seldom daunted by appearances.

He let his gaze flicker towards Ichabod's father, and spoke in a deliberately loud voice. "I was just about to offer the kid a thousand dollars for it."

At that even Ichabod forgot to cry for several seconds,

while his father—one hand on the boy's shoulder in a melodramatically protective pose—gave an audible gasp.

Brother Mark took a pace back, horrified. "You'd buy and sell a relic of the angels?" he thundered. "Who are you—apart from being an ignorant blasphemer, which is obvious?"

"I'm Den Radcliffe. Maybe you've seen my place back towards Gradyville. It's not easy to overlook. About twenty times bigger than that hovel you miscall a church."

At hearing his sect's headquarters dismissed as a hovel, Brother Mark was nettled. He tried not to show it, but it was plain from the sanctimonious tone of his answer.

"What need do we have of splendid churches when the very hosts of heaven have built a temple for us?"

"I never saw you or your followers going in there for Sunday service," Radcliffe gibed.

"We shall enter in due time, when we are cleansed of our earthly pollution," Brother Mark snapped. "You of course will go to hell—though you could gain grace by handing over that relic. Its proper place is in my church. You defile it even by looking at it, let alone touching it!"

Radcliffe tossed the ball casually into the air and caught it again. He shook his head. "I'm not going to part with it. I'm licensed by Governor Grady to be in possession of things like this, and you're not. I'll pay a fair price, but I won't let it go."

"But it's mine!" wailed Ichabod, leaving his father's side. "It's not fair! It's mine, and I won't let you take it away! They took the other one, and—and they didn't even give me any of the money!"

His father rushed after him and clamped a hand over his mouth, fractionally too late. Brother Mark had heard the betraying words.

"Greg Sims!" he rasped. "Has your boy found a relic before?"

Sims moved his feet in the dirt like an embarrassed child. He said, looking at the ground, "Well—uh—"

"Yes or no?" Brother Mark blasted.

"Well. . . Well—yes."

"A bright and shining relic of the angels?"

Sims nodded miserably. "But it wasn't my idea—it was Martha's." The flood of self-justification came with a rush. "I said give it to the church but Martha said no, tithe it if you like but we must have food and new clothes. I did pay the tithe on it, I swear! Paid the whole twelve dollars!"

"Who bought it off you—this unclean sinner here?"

"No, it was a man called Corey Bennett. He made the sign you taught us and said he follows you—"

"No disciple of mine would sell a holy relic for dirty, disgusting *money!*" roared Brother Mark. He flung out his arm, like an angel ordering Adam and Eve to quit Eden. "Go!"

Shocked murmurs were heard from the other relidges; they drew aside as from lepers. Sims, clutching his son's hand, tried to argue, but Brother Mark would have none of that.

"I said go!" he repeated. "And take the boy with you! He must be a vessel of evil, or he'd have brought what he found direct to me!"

Catching Gabe's eye, Radcliffe nodded towards Sims. Gabe understood, and as the father and son trudged dejectedly away he followed them. At a discreet distance he invited them to halt, and they complied and stood waiting. So far, so good. Anybody, child or adult, who could find two live relics was worth investigation.

"Now do you give that sacred object over?" boomed Brother Mark. "Or must I call on angels to visit you with all the plagues of Egypt?"

"Call the angels as much as you like," Radcliffe answered. "I'm going to buy this off the Sims family. If you're going to throw them out of the church, they'll need funds to keep them, I guess. You don't come into it at all."

"Then I curse you!" Brother Mark shouted, and his fingers curled over like claws. But Radcliffe, his expression bored, merely tossed the gleaming ball high in the air again—higher than before, higher in fact than he had intended.

Much higher.

The shock was fearful. He looked at where the ball ought to be. It wasn't. And it had not come down. Only a stain of radiance in the air suggested that it had ever existed.

Vanished!

"I—" whispered Brother Mark, his eyes bulging. "I curse—"

"Oh my God!" cried one of Radcliffe's men, and turned and ran.

Radcliffe stood frozen for long moments. He was recalled to awareness of the relidges' hasty departure by a fist pummelling at his arm. It was Ichabod, hysterical with fury. Radcliffe tried to brush him aside, but he persisted.

"Give it back!" he wailed. "It's mine, it's mine! I want it back!"

"Ichabod, you dirty little sinner!" his father bellowed, stumbling after him through the darkness.

"Leave him be, Mr.—Mr. Sims, isn't it?" Radcliffe recovered his self-possession with an effort. "I want to talk to you. I gather your son found one of these relics before."

"Uh. . .yes, sir, he did."

"A hundred and twenty dollars and you didn't give me a cent" moaned Ichabod. Sims cuffed him into silence.

"Was the other one like tonight's?" Radcliffe continued.

"More like a long thin egg, I guess you'd say."

"No, I mean did it shine with its own light?"

"Oh, sure. Like the ones they have in the church."

Radcliffe swallowed hard and tried to slow the pounding of his heart. The disappearance of the shining ball had shaken him, but he was getting over it. After all, just because no live relic had been reported as vanishing before didn't mean there was anything frightening about it. It could well be that the aliens had tossed it out—he remembered Gabe's question—because they knew it was near the end of its useful life, due to go pop like a perished balloon.

Yes, that argument made excellent sense. And the crucial fact remained: Ichabod had found two live relics.

Also Corey Bennett had secured the other one for a mere hundred and twenty bucks, when its price on resale would certainly be in the tens of thousands and, if it were a particularly fine example, even higher. One of Grady's had reputedly fetched a quarter of a million. That wounded Radcliffe in his professional pride. Bennett was new on the Ground; they hadn't even met each other yet.

"Mr. Sims, I want you to come and see me in the morning," he said. "Bring your son with you. Gabe! Give Mr. Sims a hundred, will you? It's—ah—compensation. And another ten for the kid. He deserves his share."

He cut short Sims's garbled thanks and strode up the hill towards his car, repressing an irrational desire to glance over his shoulder at every other step for fear an alien was coming after him to reclaim the property filched by this inferior species.

Rick had the use of a pair of binoculars kept in the car, but Waldron and Greta had had only a poor view of what was passing between Radcliffe and the relidges. While the gleaming ball was lighting the scene they could see fairly distinctly, but after it vanished there were only dim shadows.

"Clever!" Rick said admiringly when the ball disappeared right in front of Brother Mark. "The boss is always pulling new tricks!"

On that basis they expected Radcliffe to be jubilant when he rejoined them. On the contrary; his face was dour and he refused to utter another word until they returned to the house. Then he merely said, "Rick, get somebody to show them to their room. Good night."

And that was that.

XIV

During the last half-minute before ten A.M., the official starting time for the conference, Potter looked down the long table and reflected on the paradoxical nature of the gathering. To satisfy those who were still concerned with legalistic niceties, he had had to constitute this group into a subcommittee of the Congressional Committee on Emergency Countermeasures, with unlimited discretion to coopt.

But was there ever anything so absurd? We're meeting on foreign soil. We include a Soviet cabinet minister, not to mention a woman cosmonaut and a doctor, also Russian; we have three Canadians, an American psychologist, a professor of physics born in Sweden . . .

Who, he realized abruptly, wasn't here. As the wall-clock's minute-hand closed on the hour-mark he said, "Where's Jespersen?"

A saturnine man named Clarkson, one of the Canadian observers, glanced up in faint surprise. "Haven't you heard? His plane was overdue at Calgary. They've mounted a search for it."

"What? What took him to Calgary?"

"He heard a rumor about a live artifact being offered for sale there and flew down to check on it. But he never arrived."

There's a cheerful note to start the day's proceedings on!

"Excuse me." Natasha leaned forward. At these meetings she carried on a running translation service for Abramovitch, and frequently had to have post-catastrophe terms explained to her. Potter had not previously realized how many there were. "He heard about a—what?"

"A live artifact. An alien object showing signs of activity, radiating or vibrating or something like that."

"Thank you. By the way, Mr. Potter, I should also say that Dr. Zworykin apologizes to be a little late. Pitirim has shown hopeful signs today."

The others brightened, as though they had been dispensed a careful ration of optimism, like a mental vitamin pill.

"Good," Potter said. "But I'll call the meeting to order without waiting for him. Before we get down to regular business, I understand Mr. Congreve has something to say. Mike, go ahead, but keep it short, please."

Congreve rubbed his chin. "Well, it wouldn't be easy to make it long, because there's damned little to it bar a sneaking suspicion. What I just heard may reinforce it a bit, but . . . O.K., for what it's worth. As you know, Academician Abramovitch is in contact with sympathetic members of the rump administration in the Soviet Union, and at considerable risk to themselves they've managed to relay some messages to us by short wave. I've been analyzing them, and they're very suggestive.

"There's been a noticeable slacking-off in Buishenko's advance. The government forces have held two cities which Buishenko had formerly scheduled for—ah—tactical evacuation this week. Last night's messages were even hinting at countermoves to regain lost territory. All this implies that losing Pitirim did indeed undermine Buishenko's grip on his followers. But!

"Since Buishenko set up his HQ in what was designed as an emergency Kremlin during a nuclear war, it's possible for the government to monitor his transmissions. He's using known cipher-modes and scramble-patterns. Some of the intercepted traffic recently has been . . . well, enlightening.

"First off: there was to have been a blitz-style raid with air support on the government's temporary capital in the Samarkand region. It's been called off. My assessment is that Buishenko started by assuming Pitirim was in government hands, but has recieved information showing that he was wrong."

Potter's imagination filled with a picture of the situation in Russia as described by Natasha and Congreve: the whole monstrous sprawling nation torn to shreds by Buishenko's Tartar-like hordes, communications broken, government reduced to impotence by the sheer distances involved . . . In comparison it made him feel that North America was the size of a suburban lawn.

"Two: we know that the air pursuit which followed the *Red Whale* cannot have been Buishenko's. He has nothing far enough east with adequate speed or range to have made the interception. In any case why should he have imagined that the vessel had anything to do with him? We've been assuming that some local loyalist air force commander mistook what was going on for—oh—regular smuggling, or something like that.

"But putting that together with the cancellation of his planned raid on the temporary capital, another and very disturbing possibility emerges. We suspect that a reactionary faction on the government side got wind of Abramovitch's plan to take Pitirim out of the country and determined to stop it at all costs."

Potter sighed, thinking: *let not thy right hand know* . . . Yes, it was a safe bet that plenty of the surviving high officials in Russia would judge Abramovitch's scheme by an obsolete yardstick and treat it as simple treason. Old habits were dying very hard in this new age of the world.

"Are you saying they would give the information to Buishenko?" Natasha demanded. "Surely they would never do that! Besides, Pitirim could have been taken anywhere! Buishenko cannot search the entire planet Earth for him!"

"Well, there's another and even more alarming point?" Congreve said, but he was interrupted as the door slammed open and Zworykin came in, his face a battleground between fatigue and jubilation. Directly behind followed Louis Porpentine, head of the American medical team working in cooperation with him.

Abramovitch hurled an eager question at him, and received as answer a snapped, "*Khorosho*!" That much Potter didn't need translated, but the rest of the exchange was incomprehensible. He looked appealingly at Congreve. Before the spy could interpret, however, Porpentine dropped exhaustedly into Jespersen's vacant chair and announced, "Finally we managed to get him talking!"

"And are we right?" Potter demanded.

"I guess so." The psychologist yawned cavernously. "Excuse me—they called me out at five A.M. You'll have to get the details from Alexei, because I don't speak word one of the kid's language, but what it boils down to is this."

While Zworykin explained the news to his compatriots, the non-Russian-speakers craned excitedly towards Porpentine.

"Young Pitirim *has* been into the alien city not just once but several times. What's more, he enjoys doing it, and the reason he's given for not cooperating before is that we took him away from Buishenko who allowed him to go in and out of the alien city as often as he wanted."

There was a stunned silence, except for a murmur of Russian from Natasha.

Potter said at last, "But how? Without going crazy, I mean. And he isn't *that* crazy, is he?"

"God knows." A lock of hair had fallen into Porpentine's eyes; he shook it aside irritably. "As you know, Mr. Potter—though maybe some people here don't—I've spent over a year evaluating interactions between us and the aliens. I've sifted through literally hundreds of rumors about people who've managed to get into the alien city over here and return alive. I've arranged for federal agents to enter Grady's Ground and check out the most promising of the stories. But when they tried to pin them down with names and dates they invariably wound up with a reference to some hopelessly schizoid weirdo, or else, if they fell in with a religious maniac, they were told about some mythical new saint who's now more than likely ascended to heaven in a fiery chariot. I guess there must be stories like that in Russia, too"—with a glance at Natasha.

"What? Oh! Oh, yes, many of them. At the beginning we took them seriously enough to ask for volunteers who would enter the alien city and sabotage it. But—" She lapsed briefly into her own language to ask Abromovitch a question, and resumed. "Yes, it is as I thought. Not one attempt was successful. Either the man vanished, or else later he was found dirty, ragged and insane."

Abramovitch spoke up, and she translated. "We shall not know whether Pitirim can do as he says until we have taken him to the alien city here."

"That won't be so easy," Potter sighed. "It's quite true that we can occasionally inject an agent into Grady's Ground, as Dr. Porpentine mentioned—in fact Greta Delarue is there right now."

Along the table a few cocked eyebrows, a murmur which quickly stilled.

But the difficulty is that even though Grady may not be a ruthless tyrant like Buishenko, he does exert tight control over his territory. A native American can be eased across his border with a good cover-story and preferably a skill that's in short supply there. But what cover you could invent for a mentally retarded and very sickly Russian teenager, I've no idea. Obviously, sooner or later we shall have to find an answer, because otherwise there's no point in having Pitirim over here. But I must stress that it's going to be a very tough problem."

He hesitated. "Dr. Porpentine, are you certain Pitirim is telling the truth? Couldn't his boat be—well, a fantasy?"

"I doubt it. As you say, he's extremely backward, and his IQ is probably under eighty, so it's unlikely he could elaborate such a well-detailed fantasy. But there's no hurry to devise this cover for him, you know. If we take him away from here too soon, we might very well drive him back to his former apathy. I'd say it'll be at least a month before we dare even take him out of the hospital for a walk. On top of which, as you know, he's physically unwell. Buishenko's medical services must be worse than rudimentary."

"But you're going to have to move him," Congreve said.

"What?" Porpentine blinked at him.

The spy leaned forward. "I said you're going to have to move him. For the good and sufficient reason that in a very short time Buishenko is going to know where he is."

There was a blank pause. Natasha said eventually, "Mike, I simply don't believe that even the reactionary faction on our side would pass the information to him. Or are you saying that he has agents among them?"

"Neither." Congreve bit his lip, then seemed to reach a sudden decision, and addressed Potter. "Mr. Chairman, I was going to withhold this until I'd discussed it with you privately, but I've changed my mind. I hadn't heard before that Dr. Jespersen was supposed to be flying to Calgary in search of a live artifact."

"What to you mean, 'supposed'?" Clarkson countered. "I saw him take off with my own eyes."

"Yes, he flies his own plane, doesn't he?"

"Why not? The RCAF is as short of pilots as your own air force, you know."

"I'll tell you why not. Because the search party isn't going to find any wreckage on his line of flight. You see, Dr. Jespersen has always claimed that he was born in Norrköping, Sweden. But he wasn't."

Potter felt the world tilt to a crazy lopsided angle.

"Things are still functioning fairly normally in Scandinavia," Congreve pursued. "So I arranged to have some checks carried out. I'm now ninety percent certain that Dr. Jespersen is one of our Russian friends' most remarkable achievements. I think he's a hypnospy."

He glanced around, sharp-eyed. "Anybody here need that term explained? Yes? Well, it simply means that he's had a complete artificial personality construction for him under deep hypnosis. Suitable subjects are very rare—I believe we only know of about forty cases altogether. They hoped I might make one, but it turned out that although I'm a good hypnotic subject I'm not quite good enough."

"But what does all this have to do with moving Pitirim?" Porpentine demanded.

"Yes, with the state the world's in now it might seem irrelevant, but for one thing. Among the secrets the Russian government—ah—failed to hide from me while I was working over there was the location of the report-in point for returning hypnospies. It now lies deep inside Buishenko's territory. I've no idea how Jespersen proposes to get there, of course. His plane has nothing like the range to fly direct. He may very well be shot down, or killed when trying to leave government-held territory. But I can say this with confidence: nothing short of death will stop him from returning to his base, and the only factor I can think of that might have caused him to go home and report in person is the presence of a Russian cabinet minister here, explicable—according to the principles he was indoctrinated with—solely in terms of defection. And where Abramovitch is, Pitirim can be presumably be found also."

XV

Waldron awoke to discover with some surprise that he was lying with his arms tight around Greta. They were supposed to be lovers, so the fact that the guest room to which Radcliffe had dispatched their baggage was furnished with a double bed had had to be accepted, but it had been Waldron's impression that the pose was to remain a pose. Yet here they were as cosily entangled as newlyweds.

Then he remembered why. For fear the room was bugged—a precaution you might expect a successful free trader to take in the dog-eat-dog society of Grady's Ground—they had cuddled up to whisper their comments on the awe-inspiring spectacle of the alien city. So far, quite clear. But when tiredness overtook them, they had separated, surely. . . .

And clung to one another again when dreams assailed them. That was it. Waldron felt a prickle of sweat spring out on his forehead.

Because fearful images crowded his sleeping mind—entities as bright and pure as sunbeams, cold as crystal, implacable as fate itself—he had sought comfort, child-fashion, in the warm presence of another body.

Reflexively he hugged her, not from affection but from gratitude that he had not had to be alone. Asleep, without the daytime makeup designed to suit her role as a greedy aging slut, she was more than just attractive; she was beautiful. He had not realized that before. Awake, she maintained a cool aloofness that shifted occasionally into affected superiority, and he had subconsciously edited her appearance to match her manner, thinking of her as hard-faced and emotionless.

Part of that illusion had been dispelled by what she had said last night. The alien city had shaken her as much as it had him. No amount of pictures or descriptions could have prepared a human mind for that astounding reality.

Now her eyes flickered open, and she looked vaguely surprised, but made no move to push away from his embrace. She said only, "You had a bad night, didn't you? Nightmares?"

"Yes. And you?"

"Yes. About the aliens." She rubbed her eyes as though afraid of slipping back into sleep. "Jim, are we crazy? I don't mean you and me. I mean the whole human race. Even to think of opposing creatures like them . . . !"

"I don't know," Waldron muttered, and rolled towards the side of the bed. "What I do know is that if we quit, Radcliffe will have been proved right. We'll just be rats and not men any longer."

"Why was he so bitter about it last night? It had something to do with that girl at dinner with him, didn't it? I meant to ask, but last night I couldn't think of anything but the alien city."

Waldron, face dark, told the story of Maura Knight. Greta shivered.

"Oh, my God. I assumed she was just a beautiful mental defective. Some men like their women to be stupid. You mean he made her that way."

"Obviously. Though I haven't the least idea how."

"Oh. . . Well, it could have been dociline, I guess."

"What's that?" Waldron glanced up from the case, open

at the foot of the bed, from which he was extracting clothes to hang in the closets.

"A drug that a chemist at Pfizer came up with about ten years back. Never publicized. They were evaluating it at Fort Detrick for a while. The Russians were also said to have it. Ten c.c.'s is equivalent to several months' intensive brainwashing." She shuddered. "I never saw anybody who'd been given it, but from the reports I read I got the mental picture of somebody like that girl—*drained.*"

Waldron recalled with shocking violence that last night they had worried about the possibility of eavesdroppers. He slapped his hand over his mouth in a gesture for silence, and dismay spread swiftly over Greta's pale face. Not saying another word, she rose and headed for the bathroom.

If there were spy-mikes, those responsible for monitoring them hadn't yet passed on their findings to Radcliffe. Though it was late when they emerged from their room, already past ten A.M., they were taken to him sitting at the same table as last night, a half-eaten dish of pancakes before him, a servant silently keeping his coffee cup filled, a cigarette spiraling smoke up from its perch on a portable radio, which wasn't playing.

He greeted the visitors with a curt nod, but said nothing until they were provided with coffee and food. Then he took a last drag on his cigarette and as he stubbed it addressed Waldron.

"Well, *rat?*"

"Yes," Waldron said. "It made me feel that small."

"Good." Radcliffe took another cigarette and the servant standing by was quick to light it. "I wish someone would drag Governor Grady out some night and rub his nose in the same sight. I hear it's more than a year since he last set eyes on the alien city. Too long. I go out and refresh my memory every month or so." He gave a bitter laugh. "You know, I read once that when they gave a general a triumph in Ancient Rome, they had this slave standing beside him in his chariot to whisper in his ear all the time, 'Remember that you're only a man!' " He emptied his coffee cup with a nervous gulp and waved away the servant's offer of more.

"But it's better to make like a rat than a mouse, isn't it? Rats have sharp teeth. Rats carry plague. They aren't creatures you can quietly ignore because they're too insignificant to bother about. How do you feel about it? The same way I do?"

Waldron gave a cautious nod.

"Yes—" Radcliffe tapped ash off his cigarette. "You know, when I first saw that map on the wall of your office I thought Christ, here's a rat-type in this swarm of worthless mice. Then I thought again, and decided that if you were content to waste your life in that kind of job now there are aliens on Earth, you must be a mouse at heart after all. And mouse-types make me want to throw up. We got them here on the Ground too, you know. Those relidges! What happens to us if they win out? Why, we'll spend the rest of eternity singing jolly hymns to a god who doesn't give a damn about us even if he's up there, and praising angels who are no more angels than I am!" He snorted loudly.

"Grady's not a rat-type, you know. I don't know what you'd call him. Spider, maybe? He runs this Ground pretty damned well, I got to give him that. But he hasn't been out for over a year to call on the characters he ought to thank for putting him where he is. Instead he sits in the middle of his web listening to the threads of it twang, and sucking the weakest of us dry. But the hell with him, too. He's not concerned about the future. Say, is your breakfast O.K.?"

Greta nodded, mouth full, and Waldron said, "This is the best food I've had in months. Best coffee, too."

Radcliffe gave a sardonic chuckle. "That's what comes of spending the kind of money I have. I do spend it. What the hell would be the point of saving it? Tomorrow the aliens might perfectly well decide they've had enough of us and wipe us out altogether. That's what's wrong with what you were trying to do, you know. What happens if the government pulls things together, maybe manages to regain control of the Ground? Will we be any better off? Hell, no. We'll be tailing along behind people who'd rather pretend the aliens don't exist—fooling ourselves on the grandest possible scale!"

Another servant had silently entered and was waiting by the door for permission to speak. Radcliffe ignored him.

"What we need is guts. That's all. The guts to stand and face that great shining monstrosity and say, 'Damn you! Whatever you are, damn you! We have as much right in this universe as you, and a lot more right to this planet! So we're going to kick you back where you belong, and you'll never dare mess with us again!' Agreed?"

"Yes, but—" Waldron hesitated.

"But what?"

"I was going to say I'm not sure we're capable of living up to a promise like that. There's something so completely unearthly about the alien city, as though they're not only ahead of us, but started from somewhere different anyway."

"So what?" Radcliffe grunted. "Men don't have wings, but show me a bird that can go supersonic! Yes?"—to the patiently waiting servant.

"There's a man called Greg Sims to see you, sir, and a kid with him. Says you told them to call here this morning."

"I was wondering when they'd get here. Put them in the

159

audience room and I'll be with them in a moment." Radcliffe pushed back his chair. "As for you, Waldron, I'll tell you how I want you to spend today. Wander about the Ground. Watch the mice at play. Take in one of these nutty relidge meetings. Say hello to the gamblers and the whores and the rest of them. Ask all the questions you can, get 'em out of the way. Because tomorrow I'm going to put you to work, and from then on I want you to concentrate. Is that clear?"

"Absolutely," Waldron said, and rose politely as Radcliffe strode away. From the corner of his eye he saw that Greta was having difficulty in concealing her delight. They could hardly have wished for a better break.

At Radcliffe's entry Sims jumped to his feet from the chair on whose edge he had been perching. Carefully drilled, Ichabod copied his example.

"Mr. Radcliffe, sir! I'd have been here earlier, but we had trouble last night. I got into this argument with my wife, and then Brother Mark sent a cursing party to sing outside the house and stop us sleeping, and there was this fight with someone from over the way who was being kept awake too, and—"

"Shut up," Radcliffe said, and dropped into a soft leather-cushioned chair. "What's your boy's name?"

"Ichabod, sir," Sims answered, and added apologetically, "My wife's choice, not mine. Says it means 'the glory is departed'. I never could see that because according to Brother Mark the glory has come to us now and—"

"Sims, if you always talk like this I'm surprised Mark didn't throw you out of his church long ago. Will you *shut up?*"

Appalled, Sims subsided back to his chair. Ichabod, however, remained standing, his eyes fixed on Radcliffe's face and eloquent of his resentment.

"Good morning, Ichabod," Radcliffe said levelly.

The boy turned down the corners of his mouth. "I hate you," he said. "I wouldn'a come if pa hadn't beat me first. You took my ball. I found it! It was mine!"

"Ichabod!" Sims exclaimed. "You mustn't talk to Mr. Radcliffe like that!"

"Sims, if you open your mouth once more I'll throw you out of the room, is that clear?" Radcliffe snapped. And to Ichabod, in a coaxing tone: "Now listen, son. What did your pa say when you had the pretty thing before, the first one?"

Ichabod scowled. "Said it wasn't right I should have it 'cause I'm not supposed to want anything but grace. He kept on saying that even after he took it away and sold it to the man."

Sims squirmed, but the force of Radcliffe's threat kept his mouth shut.

Something is going to have to be done about Corey Bennett. But Radcliffe kept that to himself. Aloud he said, "So where did you get the first one, son?"

"It come from the holy city," Ichabod said.

"Well, of course it did. But where did you find it? Just lying on the ground?"

Ichabod rubbed his hand on his leg and didn't answer, his eyes roving all over the room.

A little more gentle probing satisfied Radcliffe that like a good many of the unschooled kids from the shanty towns hereabouts, his sense both of past time and of geographical location was poorly developed; moreover, his bulging forehead suggested he must be retarded. He switched his line of inquiry.

"Well, how about the ball you found last night? How did you come by that?"

Ichabod was more forthcoming about this. Half by deduction, half by guesswork, Radcliffe prompted him along a chronological sequence of events that looked highly promising. He learned, in some detail, Ichabod's opinion of all-night hymn-singing sessions, while Sims sat squirming but not daring to interrupt.

Eventually, Ichabod admitted, he'd become so bored that he had simply sneaked away.

"And your parents didn't notice?" Radvliffe inquired.

"Them? Of course not!"

"So what did you do when you sneaked away?"

"Went and got the ball, what else?"

Radcliffe started. It wasn't possible that Ichabod. . . Or *was* it? Memory threw fragments at him: Brother Mark saying that his disciples would enter the heavenly city when they were cleansed of pollution, a look on Ichabod's face which had not been simple rage. He drew a deep breath.

"Now let's get this straight, son. You mean you went into the holy city and just picked it up?"

"Well—well, I guess they must have an awful lot of this stuff because they throw so much of it away, so I thought they wouldn't mind if I—" Ichabod's voice tailed away as he stood torn between pride in his own daring and the anticipated wrath of his father.

Which erupted. No threats could have silenced Sims in face of such blasphemy. "Why, you lying little devil!" he roared, drawing back his fist for a fierce blow to the boy's head. "I'll teach you to mock at holy things!"

Radcliffe jumped from his chair and caught the upraised arm a fraction before the punch landed. He kicked Sims's feet from under him and the man found himself dumped foolishly on his backside. By that time alert servants, hearing the outcry, had rushed into the room.

"Sims, I warned you," Radcliffe said, breathing hard. And to the servants: "Take him away. But leave the kid."

"What?" Sims struggled to his feet, bewildered.

"The kid stays," Radcliffe said, and noted Ichabod's reaction. Sudden wild hope had flared in his dull eyes.

"But you can't take a man's son away from him!" Sims exploded.

"It's him I'm interested in, not you. Ichabod, what do you think?" And, seeing that Sims was on the verge of another outburst: "Hold your tongue!"

Ichabod hesitated for a long moment, then gathered his courage. "Mister, I always wanted to beat pa the way he beats me all the time. And you knocked him down and—and he deserved it. All the time he beats me and sometimes he kicks me, 'specially when he's drunk. And ma's no better. Worse maybe, 'cause she takes a broomhandle to me. Uh—you won't beat me all the time, will you?"

"I will not. That's a promise."

"Then I want to stay right here," Ichabod said firmly.

"When I get my hands on you, you sinful little—" Sims began. Radcliffe cut him short.

"But you won't. There may not be a Society for Prevention of Cruelty to Children on the Ground, Mr. Sims, but from what the kid says I'm doing him a service. Of course, it's true that he'll be doing me one—" He paused. "There should be a fee for that, don't you think? Shall we say a hundred dollars a month?"

"Two hundred!"

"One hundred, take it or leave it. Well? Fine!"

And that's a bargain, Radcliffe thought, *considering he looks like a lever to topple Grady for good and all!*

XVI

"What shall we do first?" Waldron murmured to Greta, and her answer was prompt.

"Go see Bennett—what else?"

He checked in midstride; they were walking down the same long corridor with one glass wall which had been the first part of the house they saw last night. "Isn't that risky? We don't want to draw Radcliffe's attention to him."

"We know for certain that one way or another a connection has been or will be made between Radcliffe and Bennett. Remember he headed straight for Radcliffe when he turned up at the City of Angels. And it's more likely to be 'will be' than 'has been'. Unless they've got acquainted since Bennett last filed a report, at this moment in time the two of them haven't met."

Hearing the paradoxical reality of the situation summed up so bluntly made the blood rush and thunder in Waldron's ears. It almost drowned out the rest of Greta's argument.

"No, but the free traders are never short of it. Grady Bennett gets—gets displaced. For all we know he may already be involved in the actions which lead up to that. We can't miss the chance of contacting him at once just because Radcliffe might start wondering if I'm not the person I pretend to be."

Unanswerable logic. Waldron shrugged and came to a

halt at the end of the corridor. "Where do you imagine they put the car? And do they have proper gasoline distribution here on the Ground?"

"Not, but the free traders are never short of it. Grady writes contracts like a South American dictator with most of the big corporations. Look, there's somebody we can ask about the car." Greta pushed open a swinging door and called to a passing servant.

It took them nearly an hour's search to locate the address Greta had for Bennett; they had to give the impression of chancing on it, for fear that if they asked directions the news might filter back to Radcliffe. It was the only one of a group of four five-story apartment buildings to have survived the passage of the mad armies. The sight of it, fresh with paint and all its glass sparkling, was incongruous by contrast with the other three so similar and so close, but windowless and with smoke-stains licking up their walls.

"You're sure that's it?" Waldron said in low tones as he braked the car.

"Certain. Look, someone's coming to meet us. You better talk to him."

Waldron nodded, feeling by reflex for the alien artifact he had again slipped into his pocket when he dressed today. Lucky charm or not, he did find its presence comforting, a memento of his old home and his old life.

From the main entrance of the building a tall black man in tan coveralls with an embroidered name on the chest was emerging. He wore a Sam Browne style belt with a holstered .45. As he came closer Waldron saw that the embroidered name was BENNETT.

"Is—uh—is Mr. Bennett at home?" he called out, rolling down his window.

"Could be," the man agreed warily. "Depends who's asking, doesn't it?"

"Would you give him this? I think he'll see us when he's read it." Waldron handed over an envelope; it contained a note scribbled by Greta which consisted of three Scientific Service cipher groups.

The man took the note and went indoors again. Waiting, Waldron glanced up the face of the building and saw that at three of the high windows men were peering watchfully down.

"I guess they don't care too much for strangers here," he said.

"I know what you mean," Greta answered in a whisper. "I feel on edge. As though murder might be done at any moment."

Neither of them spoke again until the same man returned and curtly invited them to come inside.

They found Bennett in the penthouse, among fine pictures and luxurious furniture: a man of middle height, well-dressed, with sandy hair receding and watery blue eyes. The horrible thought crossed Waldron's mind: *so that's what color they were before they became like Morello's cherries!*

They had come to call on a dead man, and they dared not warn him of the death sentence. He was unspeakably glad that Greta, not he, had to do the talking.

The moment the door closed behind the man who had escorted them, Bennett exploded.

"So you're Greta Delarue, are you? They told me to expect you. But what the hell are you doing here? I'm in a tricky enough position without gratuitous outside interference!"

Not waiting for a reply, he waved them irritably to chairs and sat down himself. "Who's the impatient son of a bitch behind all this?" he went on. "Orlando Potter?

169

He's the meddlesome type, I know that only too well. I said I'd need a full year to consolidate myself. I said it was probably over-eagerness that screwed up the last two agents you sent in. Here I am standing in dead men's shoes, damn it! And I've only been here about four and a half months, and here you come, charging in like a herd of buffalo and more than likely leaving a trail a mile wide that anybody with the brains of a mosquito could follow! Am I right about Potter?"

"Yes," Greta said in a tight voice, sitting very straight on the edge of her chair, her hands white-knuckled in her lap.

"I was sure of it. That slick-tongued bastard with his Committee on Emergency Countermeasures and all that garbage . . . Listen, I may not have been on the Ground very long, but I've been around long enough to realize one thing. All these so-called 'countermeasures' are make-believe. Fairytales designed to help people kid themselves that we can put the world back together and carry right on as though the aliens don't exist." He gave a scornful snort. "Hell, it may very well be possible, I admit that. There they sit and ignore us except when we try and attack them, and even then—well, do they actually pay attention to us, or do they simply hang up a few extra flystrips?"

Bennett must have been boiling up to this for a long time, Waldron decided. He exchanged glances with Greta, who moved one eyebrow to signal that they should let him talk himself out before trying to argue.

Leaning back in his chair, he glanced around the room while Bennett concluded his tirade. According to his sketchy briefing, Bennett had come here in the guise of a former insurance salesman. Insurance, notoriously, had foundered in the aftermath of the aliens' arrival. He was in fact a physicist with a good research record, and there were few such people left because so many universities and large laboratories had been in urban fallout zones. His orders were to apply for a free trader's license—Grady issued the licenses—and buy in all the artifacts he could, using government funds, to try and complete the only alien device ever to fall into human hands whose function seemed in the least comprehensible—or, if not its function, at any rate the pattern in which its parts ought to be arranged.

He'd done well. Moreover he had displayed considerable talent for his adopted role. He controlled this building, he had a staff of over twenty, and—as was clear from the lavish appointments of this penthouse—he enjoyed a very comfortable existence after a remarkably short time.

"We'd get somewhere if we only kept our priorities straight!" he was declaring. "I've said this again and again in my reports. We're wasting our scientific resources by deploying them so thinly. You know, some of the stuff I've seen imported to the Ground recently makes me *sick*. Thirty-nine-inch color TV sets! Fruit machines and one-armed bandits! My God, Grady bought himself a chess-playing computer the other day! That sort of thing takes precious skills away from the only job we ought to be doing—studying the aliens!"

He jumped to his feet and began to pace back and forth. "Here I am working by myself, not even allowed to know how many other federal agents we've got here, and all around me I see people trading in things that could offer us invaluable data. I don't mind so much about the corporation scientists. I'm friendly with quite a few of them, in fact. I know what they buy up does find its way back to labs with decent facilities, even though their bosses hope to make a fortune before they pass on what they learn. Nonetheless the situation's ridiculous. They passed that bill saying alien artifacts were federal property, and no one takes a blind bit of notice, so we may very possibly have the separate parts of a workable device sitting in three different labs this very minute. But what makes me want to puke all over the floor is seeing ignorant bastards like Grady and Radcliffe and the rest just grabbing what they can and selling for all the market will stand. Listen, the other day I salvaged something I hadn't expected to find in less than a year's hunting. I say salvaged, because if Grady got hold of it he'd sell it for jewelery! But it's a working artifact, damn it, and—"

He broke off. "I don't have any business saying that," he corrected himself morosely. "We don't even know whether what the aliens build can be said to *work* in any human sense."

"But according to your reports," Greta said, "you think you're on the verge of confirming that they do."

Bennett hesitated. At length, with a nod, he resumed his chair.

"I think and hope I may be. You see, ever since I arrived here I've been trying to force myself into a different frame of reference. I've been after an intuitive understanding of our relationship with the aliens. A mathematician would probably be better equipped for the job than a physicist like me, but. . . Well, a few weeks ago I had a dream about something I haven't thought of since I was a kid. My family had a weekend place in the mountains, and they build a new freeway that ran right past the end of our land. And the first winter the road was in use, there was a fatal smash on an icy downgrade. They found a fox tangled up in the wreckage. So they went out and shot his mate and cubs. The more I think about that dream, the more I come to believe my subconscious is telling me something very important. I think these so-called 'cities' are nothing of the kind. I think they're interstellar transport nexi."

Greta whistled. "It could fit," she said, staring into nowhere. "I've seen reports that mention intense gravitational disturbances—intense by comparison with the regular shift due to tides, for instance, though still only detectable with sensitive instruments."

"I wish to God they'd send me reports like that," Bennett said savagely. "Your precious Mr. Potter is ready enough to interfere with my work, but he does damned little to help it along. Ever since I hit on this hypothesis I've been asking for data about the color-patterns in the cities, because if I'm right there ought to be recurrent cycles and maybe synchronicity between various points on Earth. But I can't get an answer."

"That's not altogether surprising," Greta countered. "I mean, the fact that we can get this close to the city here is pure accident. In Russia, Buishenko would shoot down any government scientist who tried to tackle the job. So would Neveira in Brazil, and there's dense jungle in the way there too, while in Australia—"

"I know, I know. Waterless desert!" Bennett sighed. "And in Antarctica there's literally nobody at all. Oh, well: maybe when we've convinced people that there is a chance of comprehending what the aliens do, we'll get some action. And with luck it won't be long before that happens."

Waldron tensed. So did Greta, who said, "Something to do with the live artifact you just mentioned?"

"Exactly. Down in my basement strong-room—it is a strong-room, and of course everyone assumes that's all it is, when in fact it's a pretty fair lab, apart from my having to work in there by candlelight because it might attract attention if I drew power for lamps as well as the instruments I have . . . . Well, right in there I have—"

A buzzer sounded. Automatically Waldron and Greta looked around for a phone. It proved to be concealed in the chair where Bennett was sitting. He spoke to its back.

"What is it?"

"Anne Street lookout here, Mr. Bennett. Two big limousines coming this way. Mercedes like the ones Den Radcliffe owns. . . Yes, they're his O.K. I just got a clear sight of them."

Bennett started. "Radcliffe! What the hell can he want? Unless . . . Oh, no!" He jumped to his feet.

"What's wrong?" Waldron demanded.

"If Radcliffe's heard about that live artifact I bought. . . It was too precious to report to Grady, you see, so I didn't pay the duty on it. It would have wrecked my pose if they'd started wondering why I didn't resell it for jewelery. I hope to God that's not what brings him here. There are some swine on the Ground—like Grady himself—but Radcliffe is a self-styled rat, and he's determined to topple Grady regardless of who gets trodden on. You've heard about him, I guess?"

Waldron and Greta exchanged glances. "We—we know him," Greta said. "It was because he decided to hire Jim that I got the cover I'm using."

"You're working for him?" All the color drained from Bennett's face. "Then get out—fast! Before he comes in sight of the building and recognizes you or your car! Christ, I knew this was a mess when you said Potter was behind it, and now I have Radcliffe on my back because of you!"

"We made sure we weren't followed!" Waldron flared. "And we checked the car for bugs!"

"Stuff your excuses! Move, both of you! Get lost—and don't come back, or I swear I'll have my sentries gun you down!"

XVII

"Could they have spotted us?" Waldron whispered. Consciously he knew it was absurd to keep his voice down, but it seemed natural.

Twisting around to peer through the rear window, Greta said, "I don't think so, but I can't be sure."

"We'd better get well clear anyhow," Waldron said, and swung the car around a sharp corner with a screech of tire rubber. "How the hell could he have tracked us to Bennett's?"

"Maybe he didn't. I'm sure there isn't a tracer on this car, and it's a common make and a common color. More likely Bennett was right the first time."

"Yes, what was all that about evading tax on the live artifact?"

"Grady imposes a levy on all the free traders he licenses. He insists on all finds being declared. If something extra-special turns up, he tries to buy it himself so he can cream off the profit, and if the owner refuses he has to pay for the privilege of keeping it—*what the hell?*"

Waldron had jammed on the brakes halfway around another corner, and the car had skidded on a patch of gravel. Across their path, broadside on, was a large black patrol car. Beside it stood four men, all armed, in Grady's gaudy uniforms, who waited silently while Waldron brought his own vehicle back under control and halted it. Then they moved forward in puppetlike unison.

The most heavily braided of the four bent to Waldron's window with an insincere smile. "Morning!" he said. "I'm Captain Bayers. You're new on the Ground, aren't you? I don't recall seeing you before. Identification, please, and if you'll take my advice you won't argue."

Sweating, Waldron fumbled out his papers. Greta did the same. Bayers examined them carefully.

"I see," he said at length. "Hired by Den Radcliffe and came in yesterday. O.K., get out. Leave the car here. You can pick it up afterwards if it hasn't been commandeered. The governor wants a word with you. And you'd better come along as well, Miss Smith."

For a moment neither of them moved. Then, suggestively, Bayers dropped his hand to his gun.

"No, I don't want to come in and talk to Mr. Bennett," Den Radcliffe said to the black man who had warily accosted him. "I want him to come down here. All I want is to show him something."

The man made to voice an objection, changed his mind, and went back into the lobby of the building where he could be seen talking to a wall-mounted phone. Radcliffe lit a cigarette and glanced at Ichabod, next to Rick in the front seat. The kid had been washed and clothed and Radcliffe's personal physician had applied ointment to a skin condition he was suffering from—like most of the shantytown children—and shot him full of vitamins and a broad-spectrum antibiotic. He had been troublesome at first, especially at the sight of the hypodermic, but on this drive he had sat as quiet as could be wished, fascinated by the size and comfort of the car.

The black man returned. "Mr. Bennett says—" he began, but Radcliffe snapped at him.

"Hell, if he's scared to show his face let him just peek out of an upstairs window! I guess he owns a pair of binoculars, doesn't he? Rick, open the near door and let Ichabod out for a moment. That'll do."

Rick complied. Uncertain, Ichabod lowered his feet to the ground and stood blinking in the sunlight, one hand on the car's doorhandle as though afraid they might drive off and abandon him. Radcliffe scrutinized the face of the building for any sign of Bennett—and there he was, visible behind an upper window. At any rate the sandy receding hair answered to the description.

"That your boss?" he asked the black main, pointing.

"That's Mr. Bennett, yes."

"He'll go on being Mr. Bennett," Radcliffe said, and curled his lip. "But he won't be your boss much longer."

He ordered Rick to help Ichabod back in the car, and subsided with a grunt of satisfaction into the soft upholstery. He had been concerned about Corey Bennett as a possible rival for some while; the newcomer was making too much of a mark far too quickly. The sight of Ichabod, from whom he had bought a live relic which he then failed to declare—Radcliffe had verified that thanks to a spy in Grady's financial records office—could be relied on to make him thoroughly rattled. It would not be surprising if he now quietly decamped. Alternatively he might beg Radcliffe not to tell Grady of his transgression. Either way, he would never pose a threat again.

It was all working out very neatly.

Camouflaged guard-posts protecting the approaches to the Governor's Mansion shot challenges at the car over its radiophone. Bayers replied crisply and the driver did not slow down.

Last night Waldron and Greta had seen the house from a distance. Certainly it was palatial; otherwise it had appeared ordinary enough, an extravagant exercise in mock-classical idiom probably dating back to the early years of the century. As they drew closer, however, they realized it had been turned into a fortress, its façade reinforced with concrete false-walls, its roof screened with armor-plate, its windows eyelidded by heavy steel shutters poised to drop down at a moment's notice. The grounds were densely planted with hedges and shrubberies, but gaps revealed tantalizing glimpses of the private army Grady maintained —men drilling by squads on a graveled pathway, the crew of an armored car servicing their guns, six or seven tracked troop-carriers in a tidy line.

At one point the driver swerved sharply to the left, then to the right again, for no apparent reason. Noticing his passengers' surprise, Bayers chuckled.

"Mined, just here," he said. "In case you were wondering. The governor doesn't much care for—ah—uninvited callers."

And he added after a pause, "Don't worry, though. We have them set so they won't go off simply by being trodden on. Mr. Grady likes to take a stroll around the place now and then, you see. And he's a lot heavier than you or me."

Waldron feigned amusement, though in fact he was too tense to think of anything except the central question: what could Grady want with them?

Before the portico of the house, other cars were parked: one snow-white Rolls Royce, another patrol-car similar to this, and a red convertible. As they rolled to a halt, a man in impeccable clothes emerged from the house, escorted by an armed guard, and got into the red car. So did the guard, who seemed to be issuing directions. Waldron wondered how many visitors had been accidentally blown up thanks to someone's carelessness.

Bayers and his men led them to the door, handed them

over to the resident guards, and turned away, Bayers giving a mocking wave by way of farewell.

The hallway was like a Hollywood reconstruction of a Byzantine palace, marred by piles of loot along the walls. It was clearly loot, even at first glance: pictures wrapped in sacking, rough wooden crates leaking excelsior, furniture draped with plastic sheet. Armed men were everywhere, suspicious, hard-eyed.

Their new escort spoke with a thin man in a black suit. They waited while he vanished and reappeared, beckoning, then followed him down a long corridor towards the back of the house. Greta's hand found Waldron's and clutched it tightly.

Double doors were opened by yet more guards; the doors were of beautiful natural oak, with handles and fingerplates of gold. And here, at a desk bigger than the legendary Pershing desk, framed by a vast window beyond which sun lay bright on long lawns and immaculate flowerbeds.

"Governor Grady!" their escort rasped, and threw up a perfectly drilled salute.

Perhaps it was Bennett's description of the governor as a swine which had caused him to expect a gross man, Waldron reasoned. He wasn't gross. He was big, but well-proportioned: six-foot-three or four tall, with smooth black hair combed over a widening bald patch, a heavy Teddy Roosevelt moustache, red cheeks, sharp dark eyes. He wore a shirt the color of ground cinnamon; a cream jacket and a black cravat were tossed on one corner of the immense desk, half-concealing a bank of phones and intercoms.

Notoriously he was a self-indulgent man. In front of him was a tray of bottles and glasses, along with a case of eight-inch cigars and a stack of colorfully wrapped goodies, chocolates, liqueur chocolates and candies. But he did not exude the aura of a decadent feudal lordling. He looked precisely like a man capable of carving out a private empire while most of humanity was on the run like so many frightened rabbits.

He was not alone; there were two pretty girl secretaries sitting on chairs against the wall, one with a notebook and the other with a recorder, while at another much smaller desk a blond man in gray was studying the new arrivals unblinkingly. After a moment he produced a camera and took two quick pictures. But Grady's presence reduced these others to less than life-size.

"Mr. Waldron and Miss Smith," the escort said. Grady gave a nod.

"Get them chairs. They may prove cooperative, and I believe in giving people the benefit of the doubt."

Chairs were promptly provided. Mechanically Waldron and Greta sat down.

"Right," Grady said, leaning back and waving one of his cigars absently in the air, a gesture which brought the nearer of the girls hurrying to light it. "I guess you're wondering"—puff—"what I brought you here for, hm?" Puff, and a mutter of thanks. "So I'll go straight to the point. I don't have time to waste, you know. I have the Ground to run with an estimated population of nearly a million, and I *run* it, believe me—keep my finger on its pulse night and day. Or I wouldn't be here. So tell me: what's cooking between Corey Bennett and that bugger Radcliffe?"

There was silence. Waldron's mouth was absolutely dry.

"Ah, come on!" Grady barked. "I know you're new on Radcliffe's payroll, I know you left Bennett's half an hour ago, I know Radcliffe went there but left again directly because you'd already gone. On my Ground I'm like God, you know. Not a sparrow falls but I get to hear. *Well?*"

Once more, silence.

"This is your last chance," Grady said eventually. "You

182

don't know me yet, do you? You're too new here. Think you can keep secrets from me! Then listen. This morning comes in the boss relidge, the screwball who goes by the name of Brother Mark, to fink on some of his own flock— a guy called Sims, Greg Sims, and his wife Martha. Report is, they have a kid name of Ichabod who found a live relic and sold it to Corey Bennett. Bennett's a free trader. I license free traders on conditions, including that they declare what they find. Bennett didn't declare any live relic. Also I hear that last night the same kid found another one and Radcliffe tried to take it off him. Were you there?" he interrupted himself, catching some betraying reaction on Greta's face. "Thought you might have been. It'd take some special reason like inducting important new staff to keep Radcliffe away from his bedmates at that time of night!" He chuckled coarsely.

"Now today you go down to see Bennett, and you're the first birds to tangle in the net I'm putting around him. The second would have been Den Radcliffe and his men—except I thought, why the hell put Radcliffe's back up? He's a conceited bugger, thinks I don't know he dreams of the day when he'll be here instead of me. Let him dream; he'll fall over his own feet in the end. Also he hasn't declared any live relic lately, either, and particularly not the one he took off the kid last night. Brother Mark says the angels came and took it back, but he'd say that anyway. No, my guess is that Radcliffe and Bennett are trying to screw me, and I don't propose to let 'em."

He leaned in fake-confidential fashion on the desk. "I don't blame you for being taken in by Radcliffe's lies, you know. I'd be the first to admit that he runs an impressive operation. But if he snowed you with stories about how he's going to move me over, he was conning you the way he cons himself. He's the one due to go crash—and soon, too. So if you don't want to be dragged down with him—"

Waldron took a deep breath. "Mr. Grady, we only arrived yesterday, you know. Mr. Radcliffe hasn't even briefed me on my duties yet. I can say one thing, though: he didn't pick up any live relic last night. It did vanish. I guess it—well, maybe it sort of burst."

"That's a good one," Grady said. "Tell me another. Tell me for instance you just went to pay a social call on Bennett, hm?"

The words hung on the air as though engraved in fire, and no sound followed them. Waldron glanced past Grady's shoulder and froze rock-still, and knew without looking that Greta and the secretaries and the guards and the fair-haired man were staring at the window too. As though moving in deep mud, slowly and with infinite effort, Grady also turned his head.

Coming up the long sweep of lawn, not on the ground but—above? No, somehow *around* it, around any ordinary direction of travel. What? *Something.* Something hurtfully bright to the eyes. Something moving within itself without relation to its forward progress. Something as alien and as terrible as the monstrous city they had gone to see last night. . . .

XVIII

Sweating, Bennett twisted the combination on the door of the strong-room which occupied more than two-thirds of the basement of his home. He knew the door to the stairs was shut and bolted, and he had welded steel bars across the elevator shaft himself. Nonetheless he kept looking over his shoulder expecting to find that he was being watched.

There was only one explanation for the charade Radcliffe had mounted. He knew about the live relic Ichabod had found, and proposed to betray its existence to Grady.

Damn fool that I was, to lie and hide it! But what else could I have done? Grady would have wanted to know when I sold it and to whom, and if I'd delayed he'd have started wondering why, and if I'd faked a sale he'd probably have investigated the buyer because there aren't many people who can afford a live relic.

The door of the strong-room creaked as it opened. The hinges needed oiling. The hell with them. He struck a light for his candles. Crazy nuisance having to use them, but if he were to run a thicker cable than would be called for by a few lamps into what was supposedly no more than a store for money and valuables, someone might start asking inconvenient questions. Loyalties were fragile here on Grady's Ground; every servant seemed to dream of being a master, and he had had to let himself be regarded as a miser whose favorite pastime was gloating over his possessions rather than risk sharing the secret of his laboratory with anybody.

And there it was: the climax of his achievement.

When it came to studying the aliens' artifacts, conventional methods were virtually useless. They could be weighed, measured, examined through optical microscopes . . . but try for X-ray diffraction patterns and their internal structure would prove opaque; test them with reagents and even under fluorine the surface would be stubbornly unaffected; bombard them with neutrons and there would be no disturbance of the flow, as though the particles had encountered a perfect vacuum. . . .

As though they're not matter at all! What then? Energy somehow stabilized into a nonentropic condition? Words!

What could creatures capable of such marvels have had to fear from mankind's petty stocks of H and A-bombs? Maybe the equivalent of the static electricity generated by people wearing synthetic fibers, guilty of screwing up the micro-circuitry of computers!

So the only possible course was to piece random items together, with infinite patience: choose from hundreds, even thousands, of broken and inoperative odds and ends those which looked as though they might fit.

Like these.

It began with a sort of bowl, a foot across, having on its upper surface two indentations following the tautochronic curve, one larger, one smaller. The larger held a half-egg form with three more irregular objects on top; the smaller held the thin near-ovoid he had acquired from Ichabod. It was—well, it was somehow *complete,* not in a technical sense (for he still had no least inkling of what if anything it was *for*) but in an esthetic one. He recalled how his hands had shaken when he set the live artifact in place, thinking that the whole assembly would perhaps vibrate or

188

glow or—or *something*. It had not done so, and he was gloomily being forced to the conclusion that the three irregular objects should in fact have been one, combined, or conjoined, or fused. But how could they be repaired, if indeed they were broken? One could not weld, or glue, or braze, this impossible substance. . . .

No time to stand around brooding, he told himself. He had to get this prize of his off Grady's Ground, and not later than tonight. It should be in a proper government lab. All the aliens' scrap and rubbish should go to a proper lab!

He needed a crate. What could he pack the stuff into?

On the verge of turning to peer under a bench for suitable containers—he was sure he had some lying around—he checked, startled. Was something happening to the . . . device?

He stared. Yes! From the small glowing ovoid, the pattern of light was now *oozing*—permeating the bowl-like base, spreading into the larger ovoid, infecting the three objects piled above!

"Oh my God!" Bennett whispered.

For the process was not stopping when it reached the limits of the alien substance. It was spreading still further —staining the very air with radiance and taking on the shape of something as incomprehensible, as majestic and as fearful as the place from which its scattered parts had come. He gasped . . . and the inhalation drew with it some of the stained and colored air.

There was a sensation like a blow delivered to—not his physical brain, but—his abstract mind, and he collapsed on the floor without another sound.

When he woke, it was to total darkness and total silence. He cried out, and only echoes answered. Clumsily and timidly he rose to his feet; by touch he found his way to the stairs and up them to the door which was still locked and bolted. All he wanted was to get back to light and fresh air. He did not pause to grope along the bench where he had assembled the artifact and check whether it was still there.

All the lights in the building were out. No one came in response to his moans. The floor of the lobby was littered with broken glass and his shoes crunched at every step. Beyond the doors light beckoned; the neon signs were still ablaze in Gradyville. He moved towards them like an insect courting a lamp.

"There! That's him!" a voice shouted from the shadows outside, and a flashlight beam stabbed him in the eyes. Men came rushing, while he screamed and flailed his arms in vain, and they dragged him feet first down his own front steps to spit on him, and beat him, and kick him, the blasphemer who had profaned a holy relic and brought the wrath of the angelic hosts on Gradyville.

When they had finished, they threw him in a ditch half-full of wet mud.

The intercom on Potter's desk buzzed. He had been gnawing at nails already bitten to the quick and staring at the black rectangle of the window, punctuated only by stars.

They had ordered a blackout for tonight, preparing for the worst.

More than likely someone wants to know why I haven't drawn the curtains to hide the glow of my cigarette.

"What is it?"

"Air Marshal Fyffe and his aide are here, sir."

"Send them right in," Potter said, and rose to draw the curtains and switch on the lights; one could hardly receive the acting Chief of Continental Defense in a starlit office.

One glance at the face of the elderly man who entered told him that the news was bad.

"Buishenka's taken Vladivostok!" he exclaimed.

The Air Marshal nodded. "Worse than that. Better let Farnsworth give you the details—he heard them direct."

The younger man, in RCAF squadron leader's uniform, who had come in with Fyffe passed his brown leather gloves from hand to hand nervously as he spoke. "Well, sir, it's pretty difficult to get a coherent picture. Apparently there have been massive defections on the government side, and their forces are completely disorganized, so Mr. Abramovitch's contacts haven't been getting through at the agreed times. We have jamming on their regular wavelength, which suggests—"

"For heaven's sake, man!" Fyffe rapped. "Stop maundering and come to the point!"

Farnsworth reddened. "Sorry, sir. I was just trying to make it clear that we're only getting scraps of data. But we do know Buishenko took Vladivostok five or six hours ago against negligible resistance, which means he'll have suffered very few casualties, whereas we hoped he might have to lick his wounds for a bit. And, just to cap the rest, our naval forces standing by off the coast have been attacked with a new weapon."

The words took time to register. Potter felt as though liquid air had been poured into his skull, freezing his mental processes. "Something he got from the aliens?" he whispered at last.

"Presumably," Fyffe grunted. "At first, from the description I was given, I thought it must be something conventional like the 'flaming onions' the Germans used for metropolitan defense in World War II. But we've had a few TV pictures now, and they're definitely not ordinary missiles that he's using. They're large, diffuse, glowing balls that last anything up to a quarter of an hour. They seem to pop out of nowhere. They get sucked into a plane's jet intake, or drift down a ship's ventilator, and explode."

"Our reports indicate that the entire air-defense system around Vladivostok was taken out with these things," Farnsworth amplified. "After that Buishenko moved up in division strength, following a feint towards a point on the coast further north, and surrounded the city and its port. Then he dropped paratroops. But nothing like as many as we know he can call on. I'm afraid he must be reserving the rest for us."

"Invasion?" Potter spat out the word as though it had burned his tongue.

"We've got to be prepared for one," Fyffe confirmed. In the same moment the intercom buzzed. Potter snapped the switch.

"What the hell do you want? I'm busy!"

"Message for the Air Marshal, sir. We have a Cardinal on radar at sixty-five thousand feet." The voice sounded vaguely puzzled. "I'm told just to say that, and he'll understand."

"Thank you," Potter said. And to Fyffe: "The Cardinal —isn't that their ultra-high-altitude spy plane?"

Fyffe nodded.

"Can we shoot it down?"

"No, we can't." Fyffe's shoulders hunched as though they bore the cares of the entire world. "We have nothing on the whole western seaboard that could reach sixty-five thousand and intercept."

"I presume this means that your Mr. Congreve was right about Dr. Jespersen," Farnsworth said. "It can't be simple coincidence that Buishenko has concentrated all his efforts for the past week on moving eastwards."

"No, he's obviously following a lead. And if Pitirim was responsible for him getting hold of a weapon based on alien principles, no wonder he's desperate to get the boy back!" Potter rubbed his weary eyes. "So we'd better move him out of here, right away. Air Marshal?"

"I've laid on a plane," Fyffe said. "It's on ten-minute standby. Dr. Porpentine thinks the strain will drive him back to the state he was in when he arrived, you know, but Dr. Zworykin thinks he'll be all right provided he and the girl—what's her name?—Natasha go with him and keep on reassuring him in Russian." He hesitated. "We haven't been told which flight plan to issue yet, though."

"We'll go straight to Grady's Ground," Potter said. "Away from an alien city, he's an idiot and nothing more. If it's true that Buishenko has a brand-new weapon, I don't think anybody can doubt that we've got to make use of his talent too."

"But it'll be courting disaster if one of the free traders hears about him," Farnsworth objected. "I'm told they run private armies and sometimes they fight regular battles. If Pitirim really is such a prize—"

"Courting disaster," Potter cut in, "is what the human race has been doing for centuries. Should we choose to be different? Besides, what you said is only part of the picture. Grady runs his empire with a tight leash. Some of our own agents are settled there, doing research and keeping us posted, and they all say life is much quieter than it was a couple of years ago. What's more, if Buishenko does invade, Grady will have a refugee movement on his hands, and I think we can hole out with—"

The intercom buzzed again. "For the Air Marshal, sir! Forward naval units report radar contact with massive wave of aircraft, speed height and direction consistent with airborne . . . *invasion?*"

"Where are they now?" Fyffe barked.

"ETA given as plus four hours fifteen minutes."

"Four hours!" Fyffe looked at Potter. "You'd better

hurry, then, if you want to be on Grady's Ground by then. The best of luck, anyway. They call this the Age of Miracles, don't they? I hope one turns up. Because otherwise—" He turned over a gnarled hand as though spilling a little heap of sand.

"What the hell can they be shifting those troops in?" Farnsworth muttered, half to himself. "Surely he can't be building his own planes yet!"

Potter thumbed the intercom again. "Call the hospital, tell Dr. Zworykin to get Pitirim to the airport for immediate evacuation. Say I'll meet them there. And have my car at the front door in two minutes."

"Yes, sir. Uh—where are you going, sir? In case I'm asked."

"Grady's Ground," Potter said, for the hell of it. "As things stand, we're a damned sight safer dealing with the aliens than with our own lunatic species!"

XIX

Waldron groaned. The act of drawing breath for the groan hurt acutely, because all the muscles of his chest and belly were terribly bruised. But the pain was welcome as evidence that he was still alive.

He opened his eyes and saw only darkness. Something heavy, he realized, was pressing down on his legs, and at once he felt panic in two successive stages: first, thinking of being weighed down under rubble or a beam, deadfall-fashion; second, because the thing on his legs moved slightly and conjured up inconceivable horrors.

There were noises in the gloomy night. In the distance, he heard explosions—perhaps gunfire. Closer, there were scrabbling sounds, crunching sounds, scraping sounds. With slow, patient effort he identified them, shaping words with his stiff lips to make sure he understood himself: *Feet moving in gravel or suchlike, a door being forced wide, someone stubbing his toe . . .*

Abruptly there was light, so brilliant it stung his eyes, and a booming exclamation.

"So he is dead! I couldn't believe it!"

Who's dead? I'm not! I'm NOT! Waldron found his voice, deep in a throat as dry as a dustbowl, and uttered a meaningless croak.

"What was that?" another man said sharply, and then the first speaker.

"It's Waldron! What the hell's he doing here? Look, behind that pile of furniture. And his girlfriend, too."

I know those voices . . . . Oh, yes. Rick Chandler. And the other's Tony, who drove the truck.

"Get them out," Rick ordered. "Maybe they can tell us what's been going on."

Did he say girlfriend . . . ? Oh! Oh, of course! This heavy and moving thing across my legs: a human body. Yes. Greta. I—I somehow remember her as a soft weight. . . .

Figures half-seen in the clash between total darkness and tremendous glare—they had brought a searchlight that required two men to carry it, one for the power-pack and one for the reflector—moved and grasped and helped to stand. Waldron found himself on his feet, one arm around dizzily swaying Greta, whose face still showed the imbecilic emptiness of shock.

"The boss has been asking after you two," Rick said. "Grady's mansion was the last place we expected you to turn up. Don't try any tricks—I'm warning you. He'll want a lot of explaining done, you know."

"Who's—who's dead?" Waldron forced out. "Is it Grady?"

"See for yourself," Rick grunted, and gestured for the man with the light to turn his beam.

Where Grady had sat commandingly at his enormous desk, there was a hole in the floor. Bright shards of glass from the shattered windows overlay everything with a spangling of diamond-dust. Half in, half out of the hole Grady lay, his skull cracked like a boiled egg.

"What killed him?" Greta whimpered, clinging to Waldron as to a life-raft of sanity in an ocean of madness.

"You're asking me?" Rick countered sardonically. "But you were here when it happened!"

"Rick!" Tony said. He had gone closer to the body, but not to look at it—to peer down between the dangling legs into a pit which had been revealed below. "Rick, what do you suppose this was, under the floor?"

"Get the guy we caught in the driveway," Rick said. "He was one of Grady's top security men, so he may know."

There was a coming and going, and then from the direction of the double doors a man was thrust forward limping, his hands lashed behind him, his gaudy uniform dirty and a smear of blood drying on his forehead. Waldron recognized the patrol captain who had escorted them here —when? Yesterday, earlier today? He had no idea how much time had passed.

What's the name? Bay-something ... Bayers!

"There's a big hole under the floor there," Rick was saying. "What was it? It didn't get there by accident." And when Bayers didn't answer at once, he added, "Spit it out! You can see your boss is dead, so make things easy for yourself, why not?"

Bayers seemed to wilt. He said in a thin voice, "That was the governor's vault. He kept his best purchases in it. Mostly live artifacts, I believe."

"Live artifacts," Rick repeated slowly. "Yes, that figures—as much as anything does." He rounded on Waldron. "Say, what the hell were you doing here?"

"Ask Bayers," Waldron sighed. "He stopped us as we were driving around and told us to leave the car and come here because Grady wanted to talk to us."

"Is that true?" Rick demanded, and Bayers gave a resigned nod.

"I see. So what actually happened? Did you see it?"

Waldron hunted through a dazing mental fog, and images began to emerge. There had been the—the shining thing, moving towards the house. . . .

"I think," he said at last, "one of the aliens came to get his property back."

He had expected Rick to react with surprise, but instead he countered, "You mean like when the chief threw up that shiny ball last night and it just vanished. It fits, I guess."

"And the churches too," Tony grunted. Greta was shaking dreadfully; reflexively stroking her head to soothe her, Waldron looked a question, and Rick amplified.

"All hell's been let loose since you've been unconscious. The relidges are up in arms because they say their churches have been looted—you know they had a lot of live relics, and they've all been taken. Then there was this deal where Corey Bennett bought one off the Sims kid, and something happened at his place like what's happened here. We found it empty, all the lights out, the staff run off in panic, nobody around but a bunch of relidges chanting a—an exorcism, I guess. Grady's staff ran off, too. Or tried to." With a sour grin at Bayers.

"Dirty bastards," Bayers said. "No call for them to hand the Ground to Radcliffe on a platter!"

"But that's what's happened, isn't it?" Rick said. Bayers's answer was to spit sidelong into the wreckage of Grady's desk.

"O.K., let's get home," Rick said after a pause. "Can you walk O.K., Waldron? No, you look shaky. Someone give the guy an arm, someone help Miss Smith too. Move it now—the boss is going to be very interested in what they have to say."

"Orlando! *Orlando!*"

The words jolted Potter out of the half-sleep into which he had finally managed to subside despite the maddening drone of the lumbering 'copter's engines. They had decided on a 'copter for the evacuation because it was uncertain what night-landing facilities existed on Grady's Ground. The governor was known to maintain a small private air-fleet, but it consisted mainly of helicopters used for chasing smugglers across no-man's-land and a couple of executive jets reserved for him and his personal staff. Servicing and fueling modern airliners or military planes was probably beyond even his astonishing private resources, so he had not kept up his one available commercial airport, and their landing might have to be made on a highway or rough ground.

"What the hell . . . ?" Potter grumbled, then realized that it was Congreve bending over him; they had included him in the party because they wanted to have as many Russian-speakers around Pitirim as possible. He tensed. "Is something wrong?"

In a single quick glance he surveyed the interior of the cabin. Nothing was obviously amiss. Forward, the Canadian pilot Fyffe had assigned them—a young man named Stoller—with Natasha next to him as copilot; Pitirim stretched out in a semi-coma, watched over by Zworykin; nearby Porpentine was dozing, his head against the shoulder of Abramovitch who was also sleeping. Apparently normal.

"I'm afraid there may be," Congreve whispered. "Come over here to the radio. I'll show you."

Taking great care not to trip over Porpentine's outsprawled legs, Potter scrambled awkwardly to his feet and accompanied Congreve to the navigator's table, over which their radio was fixed.

"Listen," Congreve invited, handing him a pair of earphones. "That's Grady's station."

Nothing was audible but a strong hum. "Are you sure?" Potter demanded.

"As sure as I can be. We have a directional antenna. The ground-location checks. So does the frequency. So does the power output. But Grady's supposed to operate a round-the-clock commercial sound service, and since I

201

first picked up the signal I've heard nothing but the carrier."

Potter fought weariness to the back of his mind. "Uh—have you checked the other wavebands? Could the dial be miscalibrated?"

"I've done everything I can think of," Congreve broke in. He twisted the tuning knob with angry fingers. "Here —here's Federal Midwest out of Chicago, which ought to be harder to catch than Grady's station right now. Here's Federal Far-West out of Spokane. I've had all three Canadian services—hell, I've had the Mexican government broadcast out of Baja California, clear as a bell! But Grady's, which ought to be loud enough to shake the ship, is—" He snapped his fingers.

"How far are we from the Ground now?" Potter demanded.

"That's the hell of it. We're practically in sight of the alien city. Up ahead there's a faint glow through low cloud which might be a reflection from it, I guess. I never saw it before. You ever seen it?"

"Once," Potter said curtly. "After the first of our troops mutinied and turned back—the night they burned Bemidji, in fact. I was sent out to survey the situation, and I saw it then. From the air." He hesitated. "I never wanted to see it again, to be frank."

Natasha called out suddenly. "Yes, that must be it! Mike, I can see it clearly now. Can you still not raise Grady's station?"

"No!" Congreve said. And to Potter: "So what can we do?"

"Set course to skirt the alien city to the south. Keep a good distance. See if you can find any transmission at all —police band, hire-car service, anything. If you still draw a blank, we'll just have to announce ourselves."

Congreve stared. "Are you sure that's wise?"

"What else can we do, goddamn it?" Potter snapped. "Grady's proud of his radio and TV service. Things must have blown up in his face if they're off the air. I don't want to put down blind, late at night, into heaven knows what —rioting, maybe!"

"Yes, but—"

"Mr. Potter!" Stoller, leaning excitedly forward, was pointing through the nose window. "Down there—flashes on the ground. Looks like rifle fire. And there's a burning building, too."

"Sure it's not a reflection from the alien city?"

"No, that's away to port. I'm setting a course to the south—I overheard what you just said. My guess it that we're practically over Gradyville."

Potter hesitated fractionally, then barked at Congreve. "Mike, put out a call. Try the old North Dakota State Police frequency—we know Grady uses that. Identify us as a federal-authorized flight and ask for a landing site."

"But . . . !"

"Do as I say!" Potter wiped his face; sweat had sprung out and he was itching.

Reluctant, Congreve obeyed. For several minutes there was nothing to hear. Ahead, the burning building grew clearer, and at last they flew over it, jouncing in the uprush of hot air. On the streets which the flames illuminated, figures no larger than ants were scurrying about.

"This is worse than I ever expected," Stoller muttered.

"Look! Look!" Natasha had been peering into the darkness with binoculars; now she was pointing to starboard. "It's another helicopter, closing on us fast!"

"Mike, call them!" Potter cried.

"I'm trying, I'm trying!" Congreve retorted. And in the same second, a voice burst from the radio, harsh and authoritative.

"Federal 'copter! Federal 'copter! Land at once!"

Potter snatched at the mike. "Hello! Hello! This is the federal 'copter. We wish to land at a safe site and be conducted to Governor Grady. We can't land blind in the middle of a riot, or whatever is going on. Over!"

There was no reply for endless seconds. And then, with the horrifying inconsequentiality of nightmare, a yammering string of flashes lit the dark shape of the other 'copter and a line of holes sowed itself along the wall of the cabin and the last slug of nine tore open the chest of Pitirim.

XX

It was still hard for Den Radcliffe to believe, but it appeared to be true: no one else on the Ground had made preparations against the chance that Grady might drop dead or be assassinated, and consequently the rulership of this territory was falling into his hands like a ripe fruit off a shaken branch.

He sat alone at the custom-built electronic desk he had had installed in an underground sanctum beneath his house. From this one console, he could not only sweep the neighborhood with hidden TV cameras and maintain radio communication with any of his forces, but also direct the fire of his outlying fortifications, erect barricades, raise and lower steel shutters over all the windows, and in the last resort detonate any or all of over a thousand mines.

But he wasn't going to need his armaments. Not by present accounts, anyhow.

It had been an incredibly confusing day, but sense was finally emerging from the chaos of it all. The information Rick Chandler had radioed in from his car, outside the governor's mansion, had completed another section of the overall picture, and doubtless when they arrived Waldron and his woman would fill in the smaller details.

Meantime he had the chance to savor the taste of power.

Pushing a stud on the side of the desk, he said, "Bring me some cigars and a jug of Martinis, and make it fast!"

Then he leaned back with a feeling of work well done.

First had come garbled news of something amiss at Grady's place—the staff panicking, the private army scattering, forgetful even of their weapons, carrying only some crazy tale about aliens attacking the house. That had been enough to spur Radcliffe into action. His own personal army was both smaller and less conspicuous than Grady's, but his men were still chortling over the smooth way the governor had been cheated when that consignment of valuable goods was "hijacked". Two or three score people beside himself had shared the profit on that swindle, and when he alerted them they were ready to trust his judgment implicitly.

Then followed the uprising among the relidges, sparked by another similar report, this time to the effect that angels had invaded Brother Mark's church and another or possibly several others, and driven out the worshippers with flaming swords. One rumor claimed that Brother Mark was dead, but so far that had not been confirmed.

Those of Grady's forces—chiefly car-patrolmen—who had not yet heard what had happened to him, because nobody at the mansion had dared announce the news over the radio, found themselves inundated by mobs of frantic relidges. That tied them down very conveniently.

By early afternoon a good deal of street-fighting was in progress; there had also been much looting and a little arson. The relidges had attempted to storm the radio and TV stations and inform the unbelievers that the wrath of the heavenly hosts was about to descend on Gradyville, and since late afternoon there had been no transmissions on either sound or vision. The defenders had held out until sundown, but either they had been too busy to go near a microphone, or—more likely—they were afraid to do so, just in case Grady proved to be alive after all. If he were, his vengeance on anybody who had broadcast a report of his death would certainly be terrible.

Well, by this time they had been disabused of that idea. Radcliffe's forces were in possession, and waiting for a land-line to be patched in over which he planned to announce his accession to the governorship later tonight, when things had quieted down. He had midnight in mind, since it felt like an aptly symbolic time.

The relidges had also carried out a series of sporadic attacks on the governor's mansion, but had been repelled by a handful of desperate or disbelieving "heroes" and after losing a good few dead had wandered off in disgust. Also around nightfall, Rick and his men had moved in and disarmed the defenders, who were well aware by then that Grady was in fact dead.

Other relidges, with the plain intention of visiting Brother Mark's curse of last night on its designated victim —since the angels seemed to have got hold of the wrong end of the stick—had marched on Radcliffe's own home. But they had easily been beaten off. It was from wounded survivors that he had obtained a great part of his information about the day's events.

Still other relidges had made for Corey Bennett's place, and there they had not met with such a hot reception. Radcliffe regarded Bennett as the most likely among the smaller free traders to keep his head and try to profit by the crisis; after what had happened this morning, moreover, his wits would very probably be at their sharpest. But when a party of his men warily approached Bennett's home after dark they found the building empty, and a gang of relidges chanting hymns on the sidewalk nearby, smug in their belief that proper vengeance had been wrought on its former owner.

And not one of the other free traders seemed to have

reacted positively to the challenge. Radcliffe chuckled aloud—and then grew grave. It was as though a voice had whispered in his ear the phrase he had quoted to Waldron: "Remember you're only a man!"

Yes, I must drive out and look at the alien city as soon as it's safe for me to leave here. If we've finally provoked the aliens into paying attention to us, I may not enjoy my inheritance for long.

Angrily he tried to stifle the thought. He wanted to relish his success at least for a few hours. When a knock came at the door he welcomed it, shouting loudly, "Come in!"

And here, bringing a box of cigars and a jug and glass and bowl of olives on a tray, unclothed as he had ordered her to remain unless told otherwise . . . Maura Knight.

Wordlessly she set the tray down at his side, and stood back, looking hopeful. Of . . . ? Praise, possibly. Or even punishment. Just so long as he paid her attention. That was her sole reward for living now.

He stared at her, and as though a maggot were gnawing at his brain he felt his triumph turn bitter and putrid. He recalled how he had told Waldron that he was going to get what he'd paid for, one way or another. And he'd done that. She would never refuse him anything for the rest of her life.

Yet he felt cheated. Awareness of that fact had begun to claw its way up from his subconscious yesterday, when he learned that Waldron was on the Ground; that was why he had drunk so much last evening. The same disappointment was undermining his pleasure at winning control of Gradyville.

What drives me? The same need people outside feel, to pretend they are masters of something, or of someone, when compared to the aliens we're mere vermin? But I'm different from them. I'm better. I admit that I'm a rat.

It wasn't enough. He couldn't convince himself. The sour thoughts flowed on:

I didn't win this woman. The drug won her for me. I didn't win Gradyville. The aliens gave it to me. What the hell have I ever done that I can be proud of?

Abruptly he realized that someone was peeking in through the door, which Maura had left ajar, and glanced around. The intruder was Ichabod, looking shy—as ever —but determined.

"Mister, can Maura come back now, please?" he ventured. "I—I'm kind of scared after all that shooting, and there's nobody else for me to talk to. I guess I'm lonesome without my folks."

What became of the Sims couple in today's riots? Did they get shot down, or wouldn't the relidges have anything to do with them? Maybe they were attacked by their former friends! They'd have been an easy target.

Emboldened, fascinated by the contents of the room, Ichabod had advanced across the threshold. With a quick glance at Radcliffe, as though seeking his permission for even such a trivial action, Maura held her hand out for him to grasp.

"You like Maura, don't you?" Radcliffe said gruffly, more to still his dismal train of thought than because he cared about the answer. Ichabod blushed tremendously and gazed at the floor.

"Y-yes," he said in a near-whisper. "I—uh—I always wanted to see a pretty lady without any clothes on. I did try once. I went around the back of Mrs. Harrison's house and looked in the window, but Mr. Harrison caught me and beat me, and then he took me off home and my pa beat me too!" He giggled loudly. "But she shows *anybody,* and I don't feel I'm a dirty little sinner for liking it!"

Radcliffe felt a blast of laughter charging up his throat. He slapped the smooth metal of his desk and whooped and gasped and hooted and almost slid off his chair, while tears poured down his cheeks and the others, at first timidly and then with gusto, joined in.

When he could, he said, "Oh, Ichabod, that's the medicine I needed! God, I don't know when I last laughed like that—*years* ago! Yes, have your Maura back by all means. Have her all to yourself for as long as you like. That is"—with sudden total calmness—"if she doesn't mind."

"No, Mr. Radcliffe," the dull voice said. "I don't mind."

And, still holding the boy's limp hand, she led him out.

A moment after the door closed, the radiophone in the desk buzzed, and he recalled himself to business.

"What is it?"

"Mr. Radcliffe, a 'copter's approaching Gradyville from the west. It looks like a Canadian machine, but someone's calling on our regular patrol frequency claiming that it's a federal-authorized flight and demanding to be taken to Governor Grady."

"Hah! They're due for a disappointment, then, aren't they? Where are you?"

"About a mile from them, sir. This is Keene, in the Sikorsky. I've been on survey duty. Base just contacted me and said to go look the intruder over."

"Well, order them to land at once. Are you armed?"

"Just a submachinegun, sir. I mean that we have shells for. We had to use up most of our ammo on a relidge riot. I guess a couple of shots will show we mean business." And a little more faintly: "Chuck, you heard that, did you? I'll close the range."

"Just a moment," Radcliffe grunted. A light was flashing on the desk now, indicating that someone was approaching the outer defense perimeter. He spoke to an internal phone.

"Who's coming in?" he demanded.

"Rick Chandler's party, sir," a voice crackled. "Bringing Waldron and the girl."

"Fine! Put 'em in the long room. I'll be with them in a minute."

"Yes, sir."

Radcliffe turned back to the radio. "Keene! I'll leave this to your initiative. Shoot through their rotor-sweep, or something. But get them down! After what's happened today I don't want any aircraft bumbling around close to the alien city—it might get mistaken for a bomber!"

Alarm clear in his voice, Keene signed off.

Rapidly, Radcliffe checked with all his outstations in succession, and received reassuring reports from each. The Ground was under his control beyond a doubt.

I wish it didn't taste like ashes . . .

He set the desk on automatic, and rose. As he made to leave the room, though, the radio buzzed again, and he hesitated. A gray cloud of doom blurred his mind, as though he had already heard the message and it was of a nature to destroy his still-fresh victory. But he accepted the call anyway.

"Yes?"

And instead of Keene's voice, it was a stranger he heard, a man almost crying, with other noises blending in: engines droning, a woman shouting, three or four other men cursing. But the man near to tears was shrieking within inches of the microphone, and what Radcliffe heard was this.

"Bastard, bastard, *bastard!* You've killed him, do you hear? You've killed the only person in the world who can walk into an alien city and come out again! You've *killed Pitirim*, you son of a bitch! Murderer! Traitor! *Mur-der-er!*"

XXI

It dawned only gradually on Waldron that something was badly wrong with Radcliffe. Shock from the fearful experience he had undergone accounted for part of his slow-wittedness; in addition, while he was being interrogated he was also being checked by Radcliffe's personal physician, whose fingers stabbed with painful precision at his injuries before the verdict was pronounced: no broken ribs. He and Greta had been amazingly lucky. Whatever force the alien had used to enter the vault under Grady's office, it had been violent enough to shatter the walls and bring the ceiling down.

And, of course, to smash Grady's skull.

Finally, however, he did realize that Radcliffe was showing none of the signs of satisfaction one would have expected. Why not? A stroke of fate had made him undisputed master of the Ground. It might take a while to consolidate his holdings, persuade the other free traders to recognize his authority and cool down the most fanatical of the relidges . . . but he had such a long start over his competitors that his ultimate victory was beyond doubt.

Yet here he was, betraying no hint of jubilation—looking, indeed, downcast and apprehensive.

Can it be that he's afraid the aliens will snatch his new power from him before he's had time to enjoy it?

It seemed like the only reasonable explanation. Naturally, however, Waldron did not dare broach the matter directly, and before he had the chance to lead up to it by a roundabout route, there came an interruption which put all such matters out of his head.

One of the many nameless servants entered, bringing an extension phone, and whispered to Radcliffe. Seizing the phone, Radcliffe said, "Yes, Gabe? What's going on?"

Waldron strained his ears in the hope of catching Gabe's distant words, but it was no good; the doctor was putting away his instruments and making too much noise. Still, enough could be deduced from what Radcliffe himself was saying.

"Where did they come from? . . . I see. Is it going to be difficult getting them away from there? . . . Damn the relidges! Run 'em down if you have to! . . . I know, I know, but I want them all brought here right away! . . . Are any of the others hurt? . . . Orlando Potter? Who's he? . . . Is he now? Do any of the others claim to be anything special?"

At mention of Potter's name, Greta had tensed and given a stifled exclamation. This did not go unnoticed by Radcliffe, whose eyes flicked to her face and remained there until he finished talking to Gabe.

"The Russian *what?* . . . What the hell have you found, a bunch of megalomaniacs with delusions of grandeur? . . . Yes, yes, O.K. Just get them to the house and I'll make up my own mind. And don't let anybody slow you down, is that clear?"

He slammed the phone back into the hands of the waiting manservant and addressed Greta.

"The name Orlando Potter seems to mean something to you!"

Greta licked her lips and sought advice with wide and frightened eyes from Waldron, who had none to give. At last she said in a resigned tone, "Yes, you're right. He's—

uh—he's on the Congressional Countermeasures Committee."

Radcliffe pursed his lips. "Interesting! I mean it's interesting that you should know that. I didn't think many people paid attention to the Countermeasures Committee. It's a farcical idea, planning countermeasures against the aliens, isn't it?"

He stroked his chin, looking thoughtfully from her to Waldron and back.

"I suspect we've only had half the truth out of you two," he went on. "For instance, you said you were in Grady's office because Bayers picked you up while you were driving around the city. You didn't mention that you'd stopped to pay a call on Bennett. Why not?"

Waldron and Greta exchanged glances. They had had no chance to consult on details of their story . . . but it would have been useless anyway, since Bayers was in a position to punch holes in any lie they used to cover up their visit to Bennett.

"Out with it!" Radcliffe snapped. He leaped to his feet and took two long paces to confront Greta. Shooting out his hand with finger and thumb forked, he pressed cruelly under her chin and forced her to turn her face upward. "How do you know Orlando Potter, to begin with?"

She jerked her head free and shrank back in her chair to elude a renewal of the grip. "All right, I'll talk!" she blurted. "I know about him because I'm an executive of the Federal Scientific Service. He's my chief."

Radcliffe let his hand fall to his side. "So that's it," he said softly. "I take it Smith is not your real name."

Sullenly she shook her head. "I'm Greta Delarue."

"Did you know about this, or did she fool you?" Radcliffe demanded of Waldron.

"I knew," Waldron sighed.

"Hah! So why the interest in Bennett? Let me guess.

You wanted to move Grady over, and you thought he'd be more tractable than I would, is that it?"

"Hell, no," Greta muttered.

"There's no point in sticking to a lie, you know!" Radcliffe barked. "Bennett's probably dead. He's missing for sure. I've had my men combing the city for him, and they haven't found a trace anywhere."

Waldron jolted on his chair. *Of course not!* he thought. *He's gone looking for you at the City of Angels! What more likely departure point into time than the day when the aliens take a hand in the affairs of Gradyville?*

He turned to Greta, wishing he could come straight out with the idea that had just struck him. She seemed to mistake his expression for advice to make a clean breast of everything. Shrugging, she told Radcliffe, "No, he's one of my colleagues. A physicist, buying in artifacts not for resale but for study."

Radcliffe spun on his heel and resumed his chair. When he next spoke, his manner and tone had completely changed.

"I thought those bastards in Washington had turned their backs on the aliens and were concentrating exclusively on their own patch of dirt. Do you mean it isn't true?"

"Of course it isn't. But—Christ, with a hundred and thirty million demoralized, hysterical fools cluttering up the continent, how much manpower do you think we have to spare for work here?"

Radcliffe pondered for long seconds. Eventually he said, "There's one thing I don't get. I've been priding myself on knowing everything about the Ground. I never had the least suspicion that Bennett was a federal agent. So if his cover was good enough to fool me, why didn't you go straight to work for him? Why all this pantomime about being Waldron's mistress?"

Greta let go the final devastating blast. "Because at all

costs he mustn't be allowed to find out that he has *already* walked into the City of Angels and accused you of—"

She broke off. In utter amazement Waldron saw Radcliffe's face turn white as milk; his eyes closed, he slumped sideways in his chair.

He had fainted.

To Potter, the events following Pitirim's death were as inchoate as nightmare. Everything looked, sounded, felt *flat,* the way he had once heard someone describe the experience of a nervous breakdown. There was no emotional depth to his perception of the gaping wound in the boy's chest, of tears coursing down Zworykin's face, or of Congreve's hysterical cries flung at the radio. It was as though the fabric of time had been ripped and clumsily darned: things were happening, but they were jumbled out of rational sequence.

He struggled to wrestle his memories into the order he knew intellectually they must have occurred in. The descent came first, of course, a tangle of noise and blood and stinking kerosene from a punctured fuel tank. They landed on a highway, with no lights nearby, and the other 'copter followed them and armed men rushed to surround them and order them out. Over frenzied yelling he had heard Natasha blistering their captors' ears with a medley of archaic literary insults.

After that, vehicles came roaring up: two huge armored trucks, their headlights like the eyes of dragons. One of the men who arrived with them was called Gabe, and took efficient charge, silencing the commotion and putting crisp direct questions. He relayed the information back to his base by radiophone from the leading truck. At the edge of consciousness Potter picked up scraps of news: Grady was dead, Radcliffe was taking over the Ground, the rioting they had seen from the air was due to the relidges, the aliens had intervened, or people were saying they had . . . It was too much. All he could think of was the mystical trust he had had in Pitirim, to whom he had never even spoken.

Packed like cattle in the leading truck, they were then carried off for display to Radcliffe. Meantime, what else might not be going on in the world? Potter wondered whether Buishenko's hordes were drifting from the sky like snowflakes, wielding the new weapon he had heard about; whether the aliens were discussing the day's events, after their fashion, debating the need to make another smashing onslaught against the local vermin . . . It was intolerable to think about such possibilities. He let his mind fold inward, passively enduring what the world might offer.

It was not until they had been hustled out of the truck and herded down a long bright corridor, into a room where Radcliffe waited for them, that anything struck through his armor of apathy. Then he came back to the present with lightning speed.

Gretal

She looked at him wanly, according him a mere nod for greeting. Beside her was the man Waldron, her associate for this assignment, recognized from a photograph. Both were in torn dusty clothing, and scratches and bruises on their hands and faces had been smeared with yellow salve. They were clearly on the verge of exhaustion.

So, too, was the man presiding over this encounter, Radcliffe himself, whom Potter also recognized from pictures he had seen. But what kind of a person was he? Cast from the same mold as Grady—self-indulgent, unscrupulous, careless of the future? Presumably. That was the likeliest type to rise to the top in this environment.

"I guess you must be Orlando Potter," Radcliffe said slowly. He did not rise on their entrance. "And Mr. Abramovitch, and Mr. Congreve and Miss Nikolaevna and . . . ?"

"Flight Lieutenant Stoller," the pilot said in a dull voice.

"I see. Sit down; there should be enough chairs. Gabe, what did you do with the boy's body?"

"Brought it on the second truck," Gabe answered.

"Have it put in freeze. I don't know if there's anyone on the Ground who could learn anything from it, but we'll make sure it's preserved just in case. They can take it to Washington later if they like."

He glanced at the newcomers, sitting down as they had been told: rendered compliant by weariness, or shock, or despair, or sane unwillingness to offend this unknown tyrant.

"Mr. Potter," he said—not looking directly at him, but slightly to one side, as though ashamed of something—"I've been talking to Miss Delarue and I've learned a lot I didn't know before. In particular I've been told that the weirdo who attacked me at the City of Angels was, in fact, Corey Bennett." He moistened his lips. "I had his place searched, floor to roof, earlier on. No sign of him. But a few minutes ago some of my men called in to say they ran across some relidges who were boasting about how they set on him, threw him in a ditch and left him for dead. He isn't in the ditch now. I reckon he's *gone.*"

Silence, except for loud breathing from fat Abramovitch.

"You're wondering, I guess, what kind of man you have to deal with," Radcliffe resumed, and gave a bitter chuckle. "You know something? So am I. I've been used to calling Grady a swine and myself a rat, and there's a grain of truth in that. But today I've discovered I don't know how to be a *good* rat! Rats carry plague! Rats gnaw power cables! Rats jam machinery and foul granaries and —and hell, they kill kids! I want to do that much to the aliens, at least, and I don't know how. I want somebody to teach me!"

Potter conquered his astonishment and tracked down his voice in the recesses of his dry throat. He said, "God damn it, we might have been able to, but—"

"But the boy you brought from Russia has been killed," Radcliffe broke in. "Greta told me about him. I wish—" He hesitated. "But you can't turn back the clock, can you? So the hell with it; I'll say this straight out. You're wrong —the Russian kid wasn't the only person in the world who could walk into an alien city and come back again. Right here in this house I have a kid called Ichabod who last evening did just that and what's more brought out a live artifact. You can have him, and all the facilities you need. What I haven't got already, I'll send for. You can make better use of him than I could in a thousand years."

XXII

Potter had slept very badly. Last night's events had made him feel as though he had undergone a displacement like Corey Bennett's and been twisted through an alien dimension. *(How? How? But it's pointless to puzzle over that for the time being. One day perhaps we'll find out. Now all we can do is accept it as one of the facts of life— say "A of M!" and make the best of it.)*

Moreover the first thing he had heard on waking was a radio news bulletin, which—after insisting that Grady was definitely dead and Radcliffe had taken over—repeated an account of Buishenko's airborne attack on Vancouver Island picked up from the Federal Far-West station at Spokane. It sounded as though he had managed to establish a beachhead within a matter of a few hours.

The son of a bitch . . . I wonder if he'd give up and go away if we delivered Pitirim's corpse to him . . . No, not a hope. He's neither a swine nor a rat. He's the mad-dog type. It would only make him even more furious.

But Radcliffe had invited them all to breakfast with him, explaining that for the rest of the day he would be tied up with urgent administrative problems, and since the food and coffee alike were excellent Potter was growing marginally more cheerful.

As servants deftly and silently cleared away plates and cups, Potter spoke up. "Mr. Radcliffe!"

Instantly there seemed to be a shift of focus, as though —once more—some dimensional distortion had occurred and what had been the head of the table was now its foot.

"Mr. Radcliffe, I gather there are at least a few scientists on the Ground sent here by commercial corporations. I don't doubt you can fulfil your promise to provide all the facilities we need, but what we're shortest of is manpower. Do you think it's worth involving people like that in our discussions?"

Oh, this automatic formality . . . ! But it's comforting. It props up the illusion that we live in a human-controlled world.

"No," Radcliffe said flatly. "Scientists can be as greedy as anyone else, and those who've come here for the big corporations are out to make a fortune if they can. I don't believe there's a single one who's genuinely interested in mastering the aliens' techniques for the sake of it. I could be wrong, of course; after all Bennett's cover fooled me, and I guess other people may be keeping up a front. But I doubt it. What about your own committee?"

Potter hesitated. Reaching a sudden and unexpected decision, he said, "Frankly, they're worse than useless. Let's face it—the people with enterprise and guts mostly got blown to bits when the aliens fired off our nukes, and what we have left is second-rate talent dragged from backwater jobs to hold the line. The idea that we might still be able to make progress hasn't penetrated to them yet; if they can stop us from degenerating into chaos, they're satisfied."

"Didn't even the news about Bennett shake them out of their rut?" Radcliffe demanded. He glanced around the table. "I guess everybody's been filled in about that now, right?"

"Yes, I think so," Greta said. "I told Natasha last night, and I presume she passed it on to Mr. Abramovitch."

"We still have not been told one thing," Natasha said.

"It occurred to us at once. What was the immediate cause of Bennett's death?"

"Our police surgeon"—from Waldron—"said it was cerebral hemorrhage." He shuddered. "You should have seen his eyes. They were all red."

Natasha translated for Abramovitch, and relayed his reply. "Yes, that corresponds with what we have found when examining the brains of what you call 'weirdos'. Naturally we have studied very few, since we cannot approach in Russia the vicinity of our alien city." She paused. Abramovitch spoke again.

"Yes. It is that name, 'alien city'. Do we believe them literally to be cities?"

"Bennett had a theory about that," Greta said, and summarized his hypothesis about transport nexi. That provoked excited nods from Abramovitch. "But," she concluded, "he complained that no one would supply the data he needed to confirm the idea."

Potter sighed. "I know—only too well. I saw the furious memos he kept sending, telling us to analyze the color-sequences showing at the other locations. He never seemed to register the fact that ours is the only—ah—city which we can get at. As a first step I did try and persuade my committee to fly a plane over the one in the Antarctic and shoot some film at a prearranged time while Bennett was doing the same here, but they outvoted me on the grounds that they couldn't spare an aircrew. What does Mr. Abramovitch think of Bennett's idea, by the way?"

Natasha translated. "It fits very well. Particularly it fits the reversing of Bennett's body. Clearly an interstellar transport system limited by the speed of light would offer few or no advantages over physical dispatch of spaceships, but given Bennett's appearance in New York at a time when he was known to be still in Gradyville we have evidence to assume the system operates in directions varying from our normal time-axis."

"It fits something else, too," Greta said. "Whatever the alien artifacts are made of, it isn't matter in any form we recognize. Suppose they aren't matter at all, but—well, coagulations of energy somehow—"

"Slowed down?" Potter suggested.

"I guess that's what I mean." Greta put a hand to her forehead, as though dizzy. "I can almost see it, but I can't put it into words."

"Does this tell us anything about the aliens themselves?" Congreve demanded. "Are they made of coagulated energy too—whatever that is?"

"Not necessarily." Natasha exchanged several sentences with Abramovitch, while all the others bar Congreve waited impatiently. "It is possible," she continued at last, "that they are not unlike ourselves. Consider: they have chosen *this* planet for their base, with its atmosphere and gravity, when others are available, particularly Mars. We may have seen only manifestations of automatic processes which to us are inconceivably advanced but which to the aliens may be as commonplace as"—a glance at Radcliffe—"mousetraps!"

"It would explain something else, too," Radcliffe said unexpectedly. "The fact that Bennett could . . . well, unintentionally make use of one of their processes."

"Right," Potter said with a nod. "Given that he was reconstructing one of their devices. Hmm! Maybe it also explains why weirdos go crazy. Suppose their time-sense becomes deranged—suppose, for instance, they start remembering things that haven't happened yet?" Apologetically he added, "It's just a suggestion. I haven't worked out the implications."

"One thing we aren't short of on the Ground is

230

weirdos," Radcliffe said. "Any time you want a few for study, give the word and I'll send you dozens of 'em."

"On the other hand," Waldron ventured, "this flatly contradicts the fact that Pitirim and Ichabod have been in and out without being harmed. If the aliens really are fundamentally like us, or at any rate more like us than we've been assuming, why don't their processes affect everybody equally?"

Reluctant nods conceded the validity of his point.

"And another thing," he continued, emboldened. "Isn't it true that some people have wandered into the alien city and never been heard of again?"

Potter glanced at Porpentine—who had so far said nothing, like Zworykin, as though Pitirim's death had temporarily abolished their interest in the world—and recalled his reference to "mythical saints who by now have gone to heaven in a fiery chariot". He started.

"Lord, yes! I wonder whether they—"

He didn't need to complete the sentence. It was obvious that the same idea had occurred to everyone. Congreve chuckled and looked at Radcliffe.

"Say, last night you were listing some of the things rats do to humans. You left out one important item. They get on ships, don't they?"

A grim sort of joke, Potter thought. He said, "You know, the more I consider this, the more I like it. The time aspect in particular. Isn't it true that our concept of time is a highly specialized one? It's not universal, by any means, even among human cultures. Maybe the aliens' attitude to time is different—so different that most people are shaken to the foundations of their minds if they risk entering an alien city. Excuse me; I think we're stuck with the name. A child, though, and especially one whose mental functions are disturbed anyway, might not . . . well, might not care!"

231

" 'Except ye become as little children,' " Congreve murmured. "The relidges would love to hear you say that, I imagine."

"There's only one way to find out," Radcliffe said. "We shall have to take Ichabod out there and conduct a test." He hesitated. "I—uh—I guess I ought to say I'm obliged to all of you, by the way. I never had a bunch of people sit down with me and talk rationally about the aliens before. It makes them look a lot less frightening. I think we've been running scared without any need. I look forward to making a lot of progress very quickly."

"It's not that simple," Potter said grayly. "We're in an island of temporary calm right now. But what's going to happen when Buishenko's forces move inland? The Canadians will do their damnedest to stop them, of course, and we're bound to send all the reinforcements we can spare to help out, but our defenses on the West Coast are practically back to the musket stage, and Buishenko has this new weapon based on some alien technique."

"What?" A chorus of surprise and horror. "What sort of weapon?"

Potter repeated the brief description he had been given, and Natasha and Abramovitch started to talk fiercely in Russian.

Ignoring them, Radcliffe said, "Oh, I know that, Potter. You needn't think I'm kidding myself. It's going to be tough for a long while yet. I've been wondering what in hell I can do to quiet the relidges, for example. I heard earlier that Brother Mark, the king of the angel-chasers, really was killed yesterday. Walked up to the alien which came to collect the live relics stored in his church, and— well, like you might expect, they say he was struck down by a flaming sword. Losing him means the relidges are like a chicken without a head."

"So why not give them another head?" Congreve said.

"Before some genuine new fanatic crops up and takes charge."

"That's an inspiration," Radcliffe muttered. "Are you volunteering?"

Congreve put his hand on his chest, startled, as though to ask: *you mean me?* And then, after only a few seconds' reflection, said, "Well . . . well, why the hell not? I'm unlikely to be any use on the scientific side, and I do want to make myself useful somehow. O.K., I'll—"

He was interrupted by an excited cry from Natasha. "Now listen, all of you! This weapon of Buishenko—it is not from the aliens!"

"Not from the aliens?" Potter echoed in amazement. "But where did he get it, then?"

"It is based on work by Academician Kapitza," Natasha declared. "When he was under house arrest by Stalin because he refused to help make a hydrogen bomb, he did research on lightning balls—no, you say ball lightning, I am sorry. From his work it was discovered how to stabilize a globe of energy in the air with power sources from two intersecting radio beams, very tight. The wavelength is about half a meter to two meters. We had done some work to make the weapon operational, but having so many nuclear weapons we did not complete many projectors. Buishenko must have had more built for him, that is all."

"I was right," Radcliffe announced into the subsequent silence. "Once you start talking calmly about the aliens, you cut them down to size."

"Don't be in too much of a hurry," Potter countered. "They did explode all our nuclears—piles as well as warheads. They did drive armies insane just by waving a wand. . . . If Buishenko's forces manage to reach the Ground, I guess we can hope for a repeat performance of that, but I can't say I look forward to it."

"Why are you sure Buishenko will come here?" Waldron demanded.

"Where else would we logically have taken Pitirim?" Potter retorted. "As soon as he's convinced the boy isn't at Victoria any longer—"

"I'm afraid it's all too likely," Radcliffe said, glancing at his watch. "And before it happens, there are a hell of a lot of preparations to be made. You'll have to excuse me. But I won't forget about that trial you want to run on Ichabod. Late this afternoon, maybe, or this evening. I doubt if I can organize it any sooner."

XXIII

As though the stars have fallen to Earth, Potter thought. *And the Day of Judgment is at hand!*

Although the preparations they had been able to make for this crucial test were minimal, compared to the scale he would have liked—with say a thousand trained scientific observers on hand—they had taken even longer than Radcliffe had predicted. Now it was full dark, and below the helicopter, which had been put at their disposal while their own was having the bulletholes repaired, scores of fires sparkled fitfully on the hillside facing the alien city, surrounded by half-seen figures standing up to sing hymns or kneeling to pray.

"Has anybody counted them?" Greta said under her breath.

Potter glanced sidelong at her. Their brief separation had returned them to the condition of strangers; they had not enjoyed real friendship, let alone true intimacy, during the months they had been physical lovers. He found that knowledge depressing. Given it was so easy for two human beings to avoid mutual understanding, what hope was there of eventually comprehending the aliens?

"You mean counted the relidges?" he said, though she had probably not expected an answer. "Oh, two or three thousand, at a guess. I don't know what they hope to gain by camping out. You'd think that now the aliens have wrecked their churches they'd be having second thoughts."

"Oh, they are," Waldron said sourly from the other side of Greta. "All wrong! They're convinced this is the final test of their faith. Brother Mark was really Christ born again, and in three days he will rise from the dead and lead the righteous into the heavenly city."

"I hope it stays fine for them." Greta leaned across him, raising her binoculars; they each carried binoculars, a recorder, and a still or ciné camera, while Abramovitch—in the copilot's seat forward next to Natasha, who was flying the 'copter—had assembled a scratch collection of instruments from loot found in the basement of Grady's mansion earlier today. "I don't see any tents," she added after a pause. "Some of them don't even have blankets."

"Too scared to go home and fetch any," Potter sighed. "In case fire descends on the shanty towns like Sodom and Gomorrah."

"In a lot of places it already did," Waldron grunted. "So most of them probably don't have homes anymore. Looking at them, you know, makes me wonder what right we have to object when the aliens treat us as beneath contempt."

Neither of them had the heart to comment on that remark. Potter, uneasy, glanced towards Ichabod, who was excitedly pointing out the fires below to Maura, his inseparable companion. Radcliffe had warned them that the boy might be afraid of flying for the first time, but on the contrary he had been delighted. Apparently his parents regarded man's flying machines as blasphemous—a usurpation of a privilege reserved to the angels—and now he was free of their control Ichabod wanted to try everything they had forbidden.

By contrast Maura looked unhappy and uncomfortable. She had been told to put on a dress, for fear the sight of her body might infuriate the relidges, and she kept fidgeting as though she had completely lost the habit of going clad.

"What became of the kid's family, does anyone know?" Greta whispered. Potter answered in an equally low tone.

"Rick heard a rumor that they were murdered by Brother Mark's followers during the riots."

"Does he know?"

"Not yet. I judged it better to tell him later."

"Yes, of course."

Forward, Congreve—who was armed with a 16-mm. ciné camera to which he had fitted the longest telephoto lens Potter had ever seen—was using binoculars to study not the vast gleaming wall of the alien city, rearing up ahead and filling the cabin with shifting radiance, but the ground, searching for the party of Radcliffe's men who had preceded them in order to clear relidges away from the spot they had chosen for their landing. Looking at him, Waldron said suddenly, "Does Ichabod have any preference about where he goes in?"

Greta shook her head. "He says he just walks around until he finds a safe place to enter. According to Zworykin, Pitirim was just as vague."

"What kind of safe place? Does he find—well, a door, or a gate of some kind? Or simply a weak spot?"

"He can't tell us. So all we can do is take him close to where he started from last night. You know Abramovitch and I came out this afternoon and tried to reconstruct his movements. The ground is fairly soft, and we found some footprints. Beyond that, I'm afraid it's up to him."

"We've spotted the ground party!" Natasha called. "Going down now!"

"Fine!" Potter answered, and by reflex checked his still camera and recorder.

"What puzzles me," Waldron said, "is that he doesn't

look in the least bit scared. You'd think after being told so often that the city if full of angry angels——"

"True enough," Greta agreed. "But he's so pathetically pleased that we approve of what he's done, instead of whipping him for it the way his parents always did. It's a hell of a thing to say, but I honestly think he's going to be better off as an orphan."

The 'copter touched down. Beyond the glass of the nose loomed the bright bulk of the alien city. From this angle Potter found that it reminded him of something; frowning, he chased and pinned down the elusive resemblance.

Of course. A calving glacier.

But a glacier transmuted. Where the pack-ice of the Arctic would be whitish, grayish or perhaps greenish as it bent to the bitter sea and cracked off its daughter bergs, this was jewel-brilliant, more dazzling than a sunbeam, more colorful than a rainbow, more fascinating than fire. At this point the ground-hue was white with a tinge of yellow, and the bands and striations and jagged flashes which moved across the surface alternated dark red, scarlet and apple-green.

"Those colors mean something!" Natasha said fiercely as she shut off the engines. "There must be meaning in them. But will we ever know what it is?"

From this close, the sheer bulk of the alien structure was as awesome as its radiance. Shivering—and not from cold—Potter kept feeling his eyes drawn back to it as he thanked Rick, leader of the ground party, for getting rid of the relidges; they were being kept beyond rock-throwing range by the threat of guns, though no doubt they would have enjoyed smashing the helicopter.

Its quantity, its volume, is what makes it so impressive. A human city might cover just as much ground, but it would be notched, skylined, threaded with streets and alleys. This is a unity, a single mass.

His companions, apart of course from Maura and Ichabod, were helping Abramovitch rig his equipment, makeshift as it was. When Rick moved away, he took some photographs and noted the exact time on his recorder, then turned to the boy with an encouraging smile.

"Well, son, this is your big moment, isn't it? But since you've been in there twice before, it should be easy."

Liar. For all we know the aliens may have doubled their defenses and this kid is about to die or go insane.

"Oh, sure, mister!" Ichabod chirped. And hesitated, with a glance at Maura, who was gazing in childish delight at the gaudy play of colors. "Hey," he went on, "can I take Maura with me? I know she'd just love it in there!"

Startled, Potter could not answer at once. Waldron had told him about Maura, so he knew her personality had been degraded with dociline or a related drug—and on learning that he had revised his originally favorable opinion of Radcliffe. But did that mean she could stand the strain Ichabod endured without noticing? Sending a backward child on this expedition was bad enough; sending him with an artificial idiot for company . . .

"Oh, please!" The voice was bright and eager, so that for a disjointed second he thought it was Ichabod's again, but it was Maura's; she was showing the first animation he had seen on her face.

"I guess maybe it would be better if you took her some other time," he prevaricated. But Ichabod set his jaw mutinously.

"I won't go!" he threatened. "Not if she can't come too."

"We're all set," Greta called, walking towards them. "He can start off when he likes, and . . . Say, is something wrong?"

Potter explained, and then had to explain again when the others, puzzled by the delay, came to find out what

241

was happening. Sweat crawled like insects on his face. He tried cajolery, and Greta tried candy as a bribe, and Ichabod remained adamant.

"Well?" Potter said at last. "What do we do? Call it off?"

"And come back without Maura," Congreve said, nodding.

"You're as bad as my pa and ma!" Ichabod exclaimed furiously. "Telling me what I can't do all the time!" Big tears formed on his eyelids, while his mouth turned down at the corners.

"Is it really out of the question?" Potter muttered.

"Yes," Waldron said, and the others agreed. "He can get in and out O.K., we know that. But she might go crazy and attack him, or get him lost, or . . . anything."

"Very well. It's an abort," Potter said angrily. "Apologize to Mr. Abramovitch for wasting his time, Natasha."

"Oh, he quite understands," Natasha sighed. "Please come help pack up the gear again."

Despondently they complied. But, just as he was about to pick up the first item of equipment, Potter glanced back and uttered an exclamation.

"Hell! They're going anyway!"

"What?" Greta spun around, and almost broke into a run on the instant. Ichabod and Maura were no longer where they had been standing; the boy hobbling in the lead, they were already a couple of hundred yards on their way to the alien city.

Potter caught Greta's arm. "No, no!" he snapped. "If we catch him and drag him back, he'll never forgive us. He already said I'm as bad as his pa, didn't he?" Feverishly unslinging his camera, he snapped a picture of the current color-patterns. "We'll just have to make the most of our chance. Mike, get your movie camera working!"

"What do you think I'm doing?" Congreve grunted.

"But there isn't a prayer of filming them as they actually go in—there's no contrast left when you stop down far enough to get the colors right. Should have brought a spare camera with black-and-white film, might give a silhouette effect at least. Say, Maura's taken her dress off again."

"Probably a good idea," Waldron said. "She's more used to going without."

Natasha, who had hastily assisted Abramovitch to restore his instruments to working order, straightened and stretched. "So now we take pictures, and make notes, and wait, hm? I do not often smoke, but if someone has a cigarette I shall say please. It will be a tense time now."

"Here." Potter proffered a pack. And went on, "Of all the damned stupid things, giving them the chance to run off like that! I—uh—I guess I should apologize."

"Well, well!" Greta said with a recurrence of the mockery he had come to know so well during their time together. "The great Orlando Potter, apologizing!"

Her tone changed abruptly. "Oh, for heaven's sake don't make a meal out of it!"

All the color had drained from Potter's face.

"Greta, quiet!" Waldron said. "He doesn't look well."

"I'm O.K.," Potter forced out, and covered his moment of shock by taking a cigarette himself. "Keep up the pictures. We want the fullest possible coverage. I'll—uh—I'll record a note of what happened."

But behind the effortful calm of his words, his mind was in turmoil.

Doubling their defenses . . . Oh, I should have thought of this before! Suppose it's nothing as subtle as disturbance of the time-sense which drives a weirdo crazy. Suppose it's simply a low-grade effect of the same defense they use against an army.

It would have to be very low-grade indeed; after all,

there were said to be almost a million people now living inside the limit at which armies had been affected.

But if there were two factors involved, one numerical and the other qualitative, so that the reaction could be triggered either by a great many somewhat hostile people or by one intensely hostile individual . . . Natasha had said that all the Russian saboteurs went insane; on the other hand, the relidges boasted that some of their number had entered the alien city and never returned.

I must think this over. Because if it's right . . .

Later, though. While waiting for Ichabod and Maura to come out again. As yet, they hadn't gone in.

"How much longer?" Waldron muttered, grinding out the latest of too many cigarettes.

"A few moments ago I asked you the same thing," Greta countered tartly.

"Did you? Sorry, I guess I didn't hear you." Waldron glanced around; his eyes were tired of the alien splendor and its ceaseless swirl of color. "Where's Potter?"

"Went to the 'copter. Said he wanted to call Radcliffe and let him know what's happening."

"That shouldn't take him long . . . I wonder what it's like in there. Did Ichabod manage to give you any idea?"

"Not much. He did talk about a long high place full of colored lights, and the shining ball he brought back was *on* something and he had to reach up for it. Might be a shelf, might be a pedestal, might be something completely foreign to us. He did make a comparison, though. Said it was like the alley barber's. I gather that was a place with lots of mirrors and bright lights, obviously a barber shop back in the city where his family came from."

"Try again," Waldron told her. "How about a kids' Christmas show he was taken to? The cave of Ali Baba was full of jewels, wasn't it?"

Greta's jaw dropped. In disgust she said, "Hell, why didn't I think of that? It never crossed my mind. Maybe I took it for granted his parents would disapprove of going to the theater. But before the aliens came probably they weren't so strict—"

From behind them there was a shout: Congreve's voice. They spun around, and froze in horror.

With the dragging, zombie-like motion of a man fighting a fit of insanity and losing, Potter was clambering down the short ladder of the 'copter with a gun in his hand. He was descending awkwardly, staring towards them while he kept his balance with his free hand on the side of the door. And his face was transformed: the lips curled back in an animal snarl, the eyes wide and glaring, a shiny trickle of drool running down his chin.

The gun rose jerkily, wavered, steadied, targeted on the astonished Abramovitch—or perhaps on his instruments; it was hard to tell. His jaw clenched with terrible effort, and a sound leaked between his teeth which might have been, "Help me . . . !"

The gun twisted, and its muzzle pointed now at his own temple, and Waldron moved.

Infinitely long ago, infinitely far away, a piece of the aliens' incomprehensible workmanship had lain on a table in his New York apartment. Shamefaced, he had pocketed it when setting out for the Ground, and it was still in his pocket, and he knew its weight and shape with greater precision than anything else he had ever handled, even his old police automatic.

He threw.

The heavy, stubby rod slammed the bones of Potter's upraised wrist with a noise like a hammer. The gun boomed, the flash scorched his hair, but the slug whined harmlessly away, and by then Waldron had followed his missile, arms at full stretch, to claw anyhow at Potter and hurl him to the ground. Close behind him came Congreve, who twisted the pistol free and kicked it out of reach before applying an expert wrestler's grip. For long seconds Potter strained to break loose; then, as suddenly as it had come on, the mad fit left him, and he went limp and spoke in a thin parody of his normal voice.

"My God, I never thought it would be so strong!"

"What happened?" Greta cried—and the question was repeated in a shout as Rick came hurrying to find out why a gun had been fired.

"I—" Potter had to swallow. "I know now how the soldiers felt when they were driven mad. I was sitting thinking through an idea I'd just had, and I was picturing the way the world used to be—messed up, sure, but halfway to paradise compared to what it's like now—and all of a sudden I found I hated the aliens. It's very strange, you know; I never did manage to hate them before, because they always seemed so remote and . . . different. Maybe it's because Abramovitch said this morning they may be quite like us after all. I don't know. All I do know is that I felt this great wave of hate go through me, and then, without any warning, I knew I wanted to kill and smash and burn. And because I couldn't hurt the aliens, I'd have to hurt you . . . or myself."

Unsteadily he rose to his feet, rubbing his bruised wrist.

"Thanks," he added. "What the hell did you throw at me, by the way?"

"This," Waldron said, bending to retrieve the heavy rod.

Potter stared at it for a long moment. At last he gave a chuckle. "Well, well! Do you know something? I guess that may very likely be the first time anybody has used an alien product for a human purpose."

"Corey Bennett?" Greta countered. And he looked at

her straight in the eyes and rebutted her with a single word.

"Human?"

XXIV

"The way I see it is this," Potter expounded. He was shivering although they had wrapped him in a blanket, as a result of the shock he had undergone. But his voice was back to normal. "If it's true—and we agreed this morning that it must be—that some of the aliens' processes can affect humans, it's worth asking what *part* of us they affect. The answer seems to be the brain, right? Weirdos go crazy, Bennett suffered a brain hemorrhage as a result of jumping through time. Leave the reversal aside for a moment; it's not really relevant. From that we can reasonably guess that the aliens may have cut out some of the intermediate stages we use in communication and information processing. Verbalization, for example. Alternatively, and I think on the whole I prefer this idea, they may not reason in linear terms at all, but in—oh—a matrix pattern. Or a field. Or something of the sort, anyhow.

"So it struck me that possibly they have an automatic detector in operation, set to measure the complex of signals in a human brain which associates to hostility. I visualize two interrelated curves on a graph, one measuring straightforward intent to attack, one for some quality like intelligence indicating that when the attack happens it won't just be the blind pounce of an animal, it'll be something sophisticated enough to cause the aliens actual harm. Now when the combined reading exceeds a preset limit, I hypothesize that a counterfield of some kind is generated to modify the pattern. It fits, doesn't it? All of a sudden I found the hate I thought wasn't in my mind bursting loose —what I'd accumulated over years and never noticed. Half a minute later, I felt as though I was under a post-hypnotic command. Like I said, I needed to destroy something at all costs. And when I resisted that impulse, I found I was turning the gun on myself. Greta, you've read up on the Ground recently. Are there many suicides here?"

"Grady never let out any figures. Bad publicity. But rumor says yes, a lot. Not that that's surprising, of course. Virtually everybody here is some kind of refugee."

"Yes, but I suspect that a lot of the deaths could be explained by assuming the victims gave way to hatred of the aliens, the way I just did."

"Something else must be involved," Natasha said, frowning. "A numerical factor, a third line for your graph."

"Yes, I imagine there is. Right now there are two or three thousand more or less organized relidges camped around here. If you exchanged them for the same number of troops, I bet they'd take off for an orgy of looting and burning within minutes. Our armies were affected as far away as Ball Club, I seem to remember. At the extreme opposite end of the scale, didn't you say, Natasha, that you actually managed to send in saboteurs?"

"Not completely in," Natasha said. "But right up close, certainly. To within a few meters."

"It fits, Orlando," Greta said. "It does fit."

"Thanks for those few kind words," Potter countered sardonically. He glanced towards the spot where Congreve and Abramovitch were monitoring the scientific instruments and watching for the reemergence of Ichabod and Maura. "Natasha, would you explain my theory to Abramovitch and ask his opinion?"

"Surely." She had been hunkered down at his side; rising, she checked her watch and added, "I do wish they'd come back!"

"So do I," Greta concurred grimly. "It's been over an hour, and we told Ichabod on no account to stay more than a few minutes. All we wanted to prove was that he could get in and out—"

"Hey!" Congreve's voice broke excitedly on the night. "There they are now, I can see them! But . . . hell! Didn't you tell the boy not to pick up anything?"

Scrambling to his feet, Potter called back, "Over and over! Damn, what did I do with my binoculars? Yes, of course we told him—after the way the aliens snatched all the live artifacts yesterday, it'd be insane to take any more!"

"Then the temptation was just too much for them," Congreve snapped. "They've each got a whole armful of shiny gewgaws!"

"Pictures, quickly!" Potter rapped, and raised his own still camera.

As he recorded the current pattern of colors, he realized that even at this distance and on the tiny viewfinder screen of the camera he could see how the two approaching figures were bathed in coruscating light to match that from the luminous wall behind them. A tap on his shoulder, and Waldron's voice, worried.

"Should I run over to them, make them drop what they've taken?"

Potter took his time over answering. When he did, it was in a resigned tone.

"Too late for that, I'm afraid. Look. And keep on taking pictures."

He pointed. In horror and dismay they watched: moving with inhuman swiftness outward from the shining city, a thing that did not need the ground to tread on, but moved as a wave moves, making successive volumes of air bloom into furnace-bright radiance. It closed on the humans, and Congreve screamed a futile warning—futile?

Not quite! Potter felt his heart leap. Maura, startled by the shout, turned her head and caught sight of the glowingness as it swooped/dived to the attack (?). With a cry she incontinently let fall the baubles she carried, so as to snatch at Ichabod and drag him away.

Being suddenly grabbed by the arm, he too dropped his treasures, and began a wail of complaint—cut short by a howl of alarm as he too saw the alien pursuer. Perhaps all the tales about avenging angels his parents had dinned into him rose to his mind; at any rate, he promptly forgot about everything except flight. Limping, moaning, he let Maura rush him along on feet to which terror lent wings.

The pursuer, by a miracle, was content with the booty. Above the random mound of artifacts it hovered; they were somehow drawn up into its substance, and it was gone—not visibly, along the path it had followed before, but in a trice.

"Thank goodness for that!" Waldron breathed, and set out to meet the fugitives at a dead run.

"Shall I carry him?" Congreve said to Natasha, who had picked up Ichabod and was crooning to him over his helpless sobs. "We ought to get back to the 'copter right away."

"Thank you—he'd be heavy to walk with. But take care. He has wet himself in fright." Natasha transferred her burden to him. "How is Maura?" she added, looking around.

"Shaking like a leaf, but otherwise O.K.," Greta reported. She was standing with her arm around the naked girl's shoulders, comforting her. "So at any rate we've proved what we set out to do."

"A pretty negative result if you ask me," Congreve said. "A couple of nights ago Ichabod stole a live artifact and got away with it, whereas this time—"

"Correction," Waldron interrupted. "It was taken back when Radcliffe was arguing over it with Brother Mark. No, I don't think our results are negative at all. Have you asked Abramovitch what he thinks?"

"Oh, he's overjoyed," Congreve answered. "Said he got a lot of 'highly interesting' readings. Now he wants all the live artifacts we can provide, so that he can set them up and see if the aliens will retrieve them too."

"Funny, the way the—the alien ignored Maura and Ichabod," Waldron said musingly. "Almost as though they weren't there. Hmm! I wonder if—"

"What?" Potter invited.

"Nothing."

But, when they were back in the helicopter and all the instruments had been stowed and Natasha was winding up for takeoff, he spoke up again, somewhat diffidently.

"Look, I'm no scientist, and I can't pretend I've followed all the theories we've been batting around today. I feel kind of giddy, to be honest. But I've been piecing together what you said"—a nod to Potter—"with something Mike said this morning, and something you said, Greta, . . . Well, I think I may have an idea. Mike, didn't you suggest posing as a new leader for the relidges to prevent some unknown fanatic stepping into Brother Mark's shoes?"

"It seemed like a great idea for a while," Congreve said sourly. "The more I think about it, the stupider it looks."

"Just a moment. Isn't it true that Buishenko owed at least part of this tremendous impression he made on his followers to the way he could send Pitirim into the alien city and bring him back safe and sound? Well, Brother Mark couldn't go in and out—couldn't even send someone like Pitirim. But won't it prove your sanctity beyond doubt when you demonstrate that you can?"

Congreve stiffened. "Hell, if you think I'd take dociline like Maura just for the sake of—"

"No, no, I don't mean that." Waldron leaned earnestly forward. "I'm thinking of what you said this morning, remember? 'Except ye become as little children . . . !' And there is a way of 'becoming as a little child'. I've read about it. It's a trick you can pull with hypnosis, called regression. The hypnotist tells you to act as though you were five years old again, and you do."

"My God," Potter said in an awestruck tone. "Mike, he's on to something. What's more, you're a good hypnotic subject. You said you were once considered as a possible hypno-spy."

Paling, Congreve said, "Yes, I damned nearly made the grade, too. Are you seriously claiming that I could be put into a trance, walk out in front of a gang of relidges, and publicly pay a visit to the holy city?"

"Greta, could it be done?" Potter snapped.

"You'd have to ask Porpentine," she answered, brushing hair from her eyes. "It's conceivable, but don't take my word for it."

"If this works . . . !" Potter was shaking with excitement. "Waldron, you've only scratched the surface of the idea. Mike said something else this morning, which I dismissed as just a bit of gallows humor, but now I'm inclined to take it literally. What he said was, 'Rats get on ships.' "

In the silence which greeted his words, a sudden tremulous hope took root in all their minds.

Much to their surprise, they found Radcliffe waiting for them personally when they landed. Jumping down first from the door of the 'copter, Potter called to him.

"It came off! But that's only half of what we have to tell

you!" In his frantic enthusiasm for the slim chance they had conceived for mankind, he found himself forgetting everything else about Radcliffe apart from the fact that he was an improvement over Grady. For a few seconds he found himself almost liking the man.

"I have something to tell you!" Radcliffe snapped back. "More urgent than anything you've come up with! Do you know somebody called Fyffe?"

Potter sobered on the instant. He said, "Of course. He's the acting Chief of Continental Defense."

"He telephoned. Said Buishenko has taken Victoria and now controls the whole of Vancouver Island. The Canadian government tried to get away by air but almost all the planes were shot down. There *is* no Canadian government now. We can expect Buishenko, according to him, no later than tomorrow morning, and he'll probably begin with paratroops. And that stupid lazy greedy bugger Grady . . . !"

"What?"

"He didn't trust his own private army. Issued ammunition to them personally. Rationed it out. He had stocks O.K.—but they're in a concrete vault with a six-inch steel door that only he knew the combination for!"

XXV

The distant voice—somehow Potter could not think of it as belonging to an individual with a face and a name, and was labelling it mentally just "Washington"—was jagged with hysteria.

"Why should anybody here give a shit what happens on Grady's Ground? Far as I'm concerned those bastards can carry on cutting each other's throats until doomsday! Damnation, don't you realize the Russians have invaded? They've taken Vancouver Island, they've wiped out the Canadian government, there's practically no organized resistance and they're flying in reinforcements as and when they choose!"

Potter tried to interrupt. The man ignored him.

"And the refugees are on the move in Washington and Oregon, tens of thousands of them, same as last time only worse because now they *know* the Russians have landed. Why should we care about your crackbrained schemes when we're in a mess like this?"

"Stop talking about 'the Russians'!" Potter barked. "I've told you, those are Buishenko's forces, and I've told you the only conceivable reason for him to invade!" Sweat was running into his eyes; angrily he wiped it away.

"It's too big! This is a full-scale military operation, not a—a bandit raid!"

Potter felt his temper strain towards the breaking point.

"What sort of man do you think Buishenko is? An overgrown Boss Tweed, like Grady? Hell, no! He's more like a reincarnation of Atilla!"

"I don't have time to listen to any more of your garbage," Washington said. "Your last chance, Potter. Do you have the guts to come back and work to save the nation with the rest of us?"

"I'd rather put up with the aliens than a bunch of blockheaded short-sighted fools like you!" Potter snapped, his temper finally giving way. He slammed down the phone and slumped back in his chair.

Beside him, Radcliffe gave a humorless chuckle. "So you finally realized how Washington looked to those of us who settled for Grady as the lesser evil, hm?"

"I guess so," Potter admitted, running harassed fingers through his hair. "What does the situation look like this morning—any improvement?"

"None at all. The best we can hope for is that when Buishenko's men get close enough they'll go out of their minds and maybe a few of us will survive to pick up the pieces." Radcliffe uttered the words with gloomy relish.

"But I don't believe they will go crazy," Potter sighed. "They won't if my theory is correct. They don't have the least intention of attacking the aliens, and the aliens apparently don't care what we do to one another."

He jumped up angrily. "It's a nightmare! Here we are on the verge of our first real breakthrough, and it looks as though we shan't live to see the benefit. I'm going to talk to Porpentine. If I'm likely to die in the next couple of days, at least I want to go to my grave with the satisfaction of having been nearly right."

"Yes, Zworykin and I have been over both of them from head to foot," Porpentine said over his shoulder as he washed his hands in a stainless steel sink. A miniature hospital was among the more remarkable facilities of Radcliffe's home. "Short of cutting them open for a direct look, we can't find out more than we know already. Apart from literally scaring the shit out of them—excuse me—the experience left them completely unharmed."

"Fantastic," Potter grunted. "So what about Waldron's idea of using infantile regression as a means of deceiving the aliens' defenses?"

"It's barely possible it might work," Porpentine said, inserting his hands into a hot-air drier. "The sort of detector I gather you're postulating would presumably register only gross mental attitudes, the overall mood and not individual thoughts. Not that I see how it could operate at all, but I'll accept it for the sake of argument."

He dropped into a chair and crossed his legs, his expression thoughtful. "The trouble is this, though. Congreve, as we know, is an excellent hypnotic subject. But people like him are very rare. If we make the technique work for him, all we shall have proved is that it works for him! Suppose it does work; suppose volunteers come forward who are averagely accessible to hypnosis—are we to send them off and risk them returning as hopelessly schizoid as the existing weirdos? Radcliffe roped in a couple for us to study, did you know? I've never been so depressed in my life."

"I guess it will have to be a matter of volunteers," Potter said heavily. "What else can we do?"

"Yes, but if the volunteers are valuable, perhaps irreplaceable, what then? And they're likely to be, you know. Good hypnotic subjects are typically of high intelligence and strong personality."

"You mean, is the chance of our gamble paying off good enough to risk reducing some of our key personnel to mumbling lunatics? How can I say? But I tell you this:

263

if Mike Congreve wants a companion on his first trip, I'll
go with him."

There was a pause. At length Porpentine said with a
faint smile, "You won't have to. Jim Waldron's been here
already, and I tested him. He's a highly susceptible subject, and if the treatment doesn't work on him it won't work
on enough of us to be any use."

At that moment a wall-mounted PA speaker said, "Orlando Potter, please. Orlando Potter. Join Mr. Radcliffe at
once. Trouble on the way."

"Trouble!" Potter echoed with a harsh laugh. "More
like disaster! Thanks, doctor. Though I'm afraid the whole
question is about to be rendered permanently academic."

Porpentine blanched. "What do you mean?"

"You must have heard. "We're expecting Buishenko to
—ah—drop in today."

"Come in," Radcliffe said, not looking up from his control console as Potter appeared at the door of his underground sanctum. "Thought you'd like to be present at the
funeral. He's on his way; we just picked up the first wave."

Potter glanced at the multiple TV screens on which one
after another shots of key points were being projected. He
said, "How long do we have?"

"Thirty-five to forty minutes. Rick!"—to a hanging
mike.

"Yes, sir?"

"How are the relidges today?"

"Sort of chastened. It won't last."

"I guess not. O.K., thanks."

"Are we expecting any help?" Potter inquired.

"Not so as you'd notice. The Canadians have promised
all the missiles they can spare, but they only have about
thirty within range. A few fighters have been harassing
Buishenko's planes, but I only know that because I picked

up a couple of clear-language calls for help on the Air Force band. Washington won't talk to us, you know, Gabe!"

"Yes, sir?"

"Making any impression on the door of that vault?"

"Two hours ought to see us through."

"We don't have two hours. Change of plan. Mine it, and be quick. Run a landline away from the charges. Hide the terminals somewhere we can find 'em again later. If Buishenko turns up in person and takes over the Grady mansion, maybe we could at least bring it down around his ears."

"Sir, two hours is a maximum. Surely we can stand 'em off for a while after they—"

"O.K., do both!"

Radcliffe leaned back with a sigh. "Never thought I'd wind up making with the *Götterdämmerung* bit," he muttered. "But it seems like the only thing I can do. Lord knows where Buishenko got all those planes of his—we counted over a hundred already, and we're not sure there isn't a second wave. Whatever we do, whatever anybody does, he's almost bound to get on the Ground with five or six thousand men. Suppose we have a drink. I got some English gin in that compartment there, courtesy of Grady's estate." He pointed at a sliding door on the side of the console. Compliant, Potter opened it and found bottles and glasses and a bucket of ice.

"With tonic, half and half," Radcliffe said.

And sipped, never taking his eyes from the TV screens.

Potter's mind filled with hopeless visions. Out around the alien city the relidges, still chanting their foolish hymns, unaware of the wrath of an all-too-human kind which was about to descend from heaven. On the roads to the west, hordes of maddened refugees, many of them fleeing their homes for the second time in less than a decade. And here, waiting for the storm to break, a handful of people who had deluded themselves into believing they could defy beings closer to the angels. . . .

Is this a case of survival of the fittest? Are we shut out forever from the clan of the highest races, those who come and go between the stars? Buishenko and those like him care nothing about the stars, and never will. Does that mean the rest of us must be content to copy them? A rat with dreams of flying is not cut out for the life of rats!

"Think there's any hope for us?" Radcliffe said unexpectedly. "I don't mean you and me. I mean mankind."

"I don't know," Potter answered candidly. "Sometimes I get the impression the spirit is being bled out of us. Ever been in a country occupied by a powerful foreign army?"

Radcliffe shook his head.

"I was in Viet Nam two or three times in the—the old days. And there were all these uneducated peasants caught up in a monstrous clash of ideologies which they didn't understand. The most advanced machines they'd ever run across were broken-down old trucks and tractors. All of a sudden, here was this war going on around them with rockets and tanks and helicopters. Their minds closed up. They had no—no handle to grasp the situation by. Their language didn't even have words for what the fighting was about So the best they could hope for was to raise a harvest and keep a few kids from starving to death so they'd be provided for in old age. That was the greatest ambition they could take seriously."

"Think that's how we're going to wind up?" Radcliffe said, and glanced at his watch. "Ah, there's news on Far-West in a couple of minutes—and come to think of it I might as well monitor any other station I can reach." He flicked a series of switches and the room filled with a gentle susurrus of sound from which occasional words peaked.

"I guess so," Potter said in answer to the earlier question. "Oh, in two or three generations we may adjust enough to make another attempt . . . but equally we may adjust so well the idea never enters our heads. Then we'll have become an inferior species. Permanently."

The radio crackled again.

"Rick here, Mr. Radcliffe. It's no use. Things are getting out of control. The word's gotten around about Buishenko and there are refugees coming into the west side of the Ground like a tidal wave and the relidges are turning out in force again and—oh, hell, by the time Buishenko gets here he'll just be able to walk over us!"

"Do your best," Radcliffe said without emotion. "What else can I say?"

"Nothing, I guess," Rick muttered. "O.K., I just needed to blow off a little steam."

"Want to be evacuated?" Radcliffe said, turning to Potter.

"Rats leaving a sinking ship?" the latter countered. "I didn't realize you had facilities."

"Oh, I've been keeping a 'copter fueled and ready. I just decided I don't want it. You have it. Take Natasha and Zworykin and Abramovitch—if Buishenko gets his hands on them he'll probably show them what he thinks of them, right? And I guess you'd better take the kid, too. And Maura. That's about the limit of what it can carry. I'll call the airfield and tell 'em you're on the way."

Before Potter could say anything, he had thumbed a switch. "Keene, you there?" he snapped.

"What? Oh! Yes, Mr. Radcliffe. Look, there's something very funny going on. I just picked up a whole string of Russian, very loud. The guy sounded like he was in a panic. Mike Congreve is over at the radar desk and he speaks Russian, so maybe he knows what . . . yes, just a second, he's coming this way, and . . . Mike, what the hell are you laughing at?"

"They're turning back!" Faint, as though Congreve were distant from the microphone, but perfectly clear.

"What did you say?" Radcliffe barked.

"Who's that on the radio? Oh, I know that voice. Yes, Mr. Radcliffe." More loudly. "It's quite true. They've been recalled."

"But *why?*"

"The Chinese! That message just now said they're invading Buishenko's territory in force."

The Chinese! Potter doubled his fists so that his nails bit painfully into his palms. One had almost forgotten about that sleeping giant of a country, which had closed up on itself again after the arrival of the aliens, in the ancient manner of the Middle Kingdom, its leaders thinking perhaps that one day when the other Great Powers had been sufficiently ravaged they might quietly reemerge on to the world scene. It seemed the day had dawned sooner than predicted.

"Age of Miracles," Radcliffe said under his breath, and for the first time Potter felt the phrase contained a grain of truth.

XXVI

A week later Waldron stood shivering on the same hillside from which they had watched Ichabod and Maura set off on their nearly disastrous expedition. A cool wind carried the sound of chanting; the relidges were still clinging to their beliefs, their numbers greatly swollen by the influx of refugees who had fled from Buishenko's invasion, and now the danger was past were too weary to go home—or perhaps afraid to face the scorn of friends who had stayed put. A score of would-be successors to Brother Mark were wandering wild-eyed from group to group, preaching on texts from the Book of Revelations. Luckily, so far no clear-cut inheritor of his mantle had emerged.

If this doesn't work . . .

But it had to work. He looked around, seeing Greta, Potter, Congreve, Porpentine, others and others. Rick had taken over the big movie camera Congreve had previously used. A short distance away, Natasha and Abramovitch were setting up a rather more elaborate array of instruments than before; during the past few days they had had time to sift through the incredible miscellany of loot accumulated by Grady, and extracted enough equipment to stock a small physics lab.

Natasha called out that everything was ready, and he and Congreve moved towards Porpentine.

"O.K.!" the psychologist said briskly. "You both know

—at the moment—how this technique works. When I give the order, you'll regress to the respective juvenile ages which you can reach most completely. You'll approach the alien city and if possible go inside. You're protected by hypnotic injunctions against taking anything and against staying too log. When you come out again, you'll revert automatically to normal awareness. Are you ready? When I say 'nine' . . . One, three, five, seven, *nine!*"

Waldron blinked and stared at the looming, shining marvel ahead of him as though he had never seen it before. In a very real sense, he hadn't. Somehow—he didn't remember how—he knew it was safe to go to it and see all the marvels hidden inside. Provided, of course, that he didn't go alone, but went with his friend Mike, whose mind was as full as his own with love and adoration for the beings who had devised such a miraculous edifice.

Not saying anything, gazing with hungry eyes at the glory before him, he beckoned Mike and set off across the rough ground.

Oh, the colors! Emerald and amethyst, ruby and turquoise, sparkling and gleaming! But—*mustn't touch!* Mustn't take anything. Look as much as you like, but *leave things alone!*

"I will," Jimmy Waldron said, a good boy aged seven excited to be visiting such a wonderful place in company with his best friend Mike who was nine.

He walked at a dutiful calm pace on the rough ground that ended abruptly where transparent air turned into a riot of color and light. Sheened and filmed with beauty, this was an elseness, not a wall. Division: here, the see-through breeze; there, the be-through frieze. It did not cross his mind to wonder how they would enter, whether there was a gate or a door or a portal. Entering had nothing to do with it. Other-going did. Some few yards distant still from the shining, which from here looked like a mist somehow prevented from drifting and not at all like a solid barrier, he experienced a pleasant shift of directions, very much like letting his body fall to full arm-stretch from a tree-bough and swinging, except that there was no back-and-forth, *only* forth.

The steps regularly measured compressed into a glide and the last/next several paces happened without being noticed. First there was a gentle sucking sensation, not applied only to the surface of his body (lowering himself into water made astonishingly viscous) but to every cell and fiber of his being: as an iron filing might feel on responding to a magnetic field. Oh, yes! Glancing back because of a last tiny tingle of alarm he saw clearly, but confusedly, as in a kaleidoscope with transfinite mirrors around it (the polygonal truth of a circle), the exterior Earth; he was reassured to know that this amazing place could be looked out of. For he was already in it. As were-in-dark into are-in-light at the touch of a switch, electricity not having been discovered yet. It made him gasp, but with delight. Everywhere happened to him, instantly! No sky no ground no horizon no up no down but only *around,* the immanence (a word he had not learned at so young an age) of iridescence (a word he had fallen in love with and proudly boasted of spelling with the correct single *r*). Oh delicious. Blue sparkled tartly on his tongue, but on balance (over an infinite abyss) he better liked the gold which was inspiriting and heavy in all directions, especially inward.

Mike said something in a ripple of predictive pinks across which black bars glossed additional layers of meaning; he was not sure whether he heard, tasted, smelled or was hurt by the information, but he understood it and awared that there was very much to appre-see-eat in very little X10shun of thyme. He tunneled back concurrence, hot brown sand fashion, and imagined himself as a waffle-iron, which was very funny. It broke him up into about a gross of separate bits.

But that was at the surface/frontier/border/transition zone/meniscus. Click, he had feet again, hands body et cetera. Here there was place, which briefly or perhaps for several eternities there had not been, and substance, which had dissipated but now was back, and he could see Mike, friend, draped (like himself he realized) in rainbows stiff as silk and rough as butter. It was too much to reason about. It was a totality, an embracing feel/sense, beyond dissection like the sudden recent improbable interest (age 7) in the presence of girls budding into body-hair and . . . (??? Age 7? An instant of confusion, if there were instants here; he found other figures like 12 and 38-24-36 and 17 washing across his mind, fraught with incomprehensible significance and ignored them because he couldn't reason about them or anything, could only experience and react.)

Fundamental, anyhow, was the number EYE. Straight ahead lay all possible directions including east, west, north, south, up, down, sideways, backwards, acute, obtuse, slow, fast, fat, thin, bronze, yellow, parabolic, paregoric and pandemonic. It was great fun.

"We've done it!" Mike exclaimed. "We got outside!"

"And look at everything!" Jimmy cried. (That was possible from where they were.) He had to giggle. "Mustn't touch!" (Funny, because touching couldn't be avoided. The place touched them, inside and throughout.) Paths, passageways, corridors, rooms, tracks, volumes!

Objects . . . after their fashion. Dreamwise, they moved without motion, being in a succession of localities while remaining where they were. Fairground: the engineer at the center of the carousel, without an engine and without the world revolving because it wasn't a *round* turning . . . No use; if he was ever going to find words, that must be later. What counted was that it was happening, and it was wonderful.

They must be objects, though, surely . . . except they were not. They—they *existed*. Like position and direction. It was possible to wander among them and examine them, often making a slight effort akin to reaching out/up/into, at other times (if any) simply chancing on them. The first was a fabulous sparkling ellipsoidal shower, at least as big as a breath and nearly as light as fever-heat. Some of the sparks were capacious and smelt of probity and congratulations. Others, though, were hollow, prickly with fatigue, and incurred a sense of being remote.

Digesting that led to vague hunger, so they agreed on a spiral under their left and front respectively (they were talking all the time, of course, being overwhelmed by the variety of impingement) and invoked it until its absolute cold began to bore them. By then they were oriented—the sunrise was among the directions they were facing—and the place began to make sense of them, so they were able to start counting the hundred paces which, it had been agreed, must limit this initial incursion. In Jimmy's case the initial was W, and in Mike's it was C.

The limiting velocity here is W.

"Well, it is for me at any rate," Jimmy said, proving it by saying a cloud of pumpkins though not quite understanding what a limiting velocity might be. Something at which you could expand outwards, he imagined, doing it. A cluster of spheroids like a bunch of grapes dangling from a hyperbolic function—well, it was curved like a cat's tail, actually—measured him off in degrees absolute and that tickled until he could scarcely bear it, although he chuckled as he writhed.

Little by little, to his surprise, the tickling began to make sense of a red fish, and the thought expressed to him: *I ought to be wearing coordinates. What goes well with red?*

Mike's answer was prompt and coarse-textured. He had sneezed about it for a while and decided on a very mild electric shock, the kind you get when you touch your tongue to the terminals of a dry cell. That fitted excellently except that it wasn't completely square, and he wriggled around until he had altered the perspective he was viewing it from. Were the hundred paces up, or had they turned minus? Counting backward, he got down to about twenty-nine or possibly fifty-five, and hesitated. The brilliance was somewhat dazzling and the style of his friend was inadequate, lacking the middle rung.

"Mike?" he called, looking up and forth the cylindrical platform he was groping down.

"Yes, Jimmy? Say, did you greet this one yet? It horns us! That must be what it's here for!"

"Mike, this way—over here!" (But where am I?) "You're going too lofted!"

"No, I'm right here inside you! I promised we wouldn't be too short, same as you did!"

What? What?

(But it was making more and more sense, because it was full of echoes: age-seven echoes. On a window ledge, nailed secure, a box with one side and the floor of wire mesh, enclosing two sad chickens that dropped limy excreta to the street. A moment when, standing at the front of a subway train, he had been sure that *this* time the brakes were going to fail. In a corner scarcely daring to breathe while his cousin three years older and much stronger hunted him, promising loudly and with fervor he would smash his teeth, kick his balls, pull his hair out by the handful. Everything on the sudden confining, expectant, apprehensive.)

"Jimmy? Jimmy!"
"Here comes a something!"

A *someone*.

August, majestic, awful, the crystallized sound of a million crashing cars made his desire fromness. Flee-shrink-absent him. He knew how.

He knew how.

It was exactly like discovering that he could wiggle his ears, which he had never thought of until he was fourteen.

But I'm not fourteen. I'm only seven. Somewhere I must have got double/folded/plied.

"The last time I went through here—"

I haven't been here before. I didn't come here until next time, was I? Oh, this is terrible, I can't stand it, guts twisting, nausea churning, *where's Mike?* The entity, the being, the personage (infinite reflections of authority from mother to master, parent to policeman): must not catch in that gong-ring claw I felt brush the raw nerve of my spine. Red, shock-taste, go back until it looks absolutely square and . . .

The way out, as before in a deformed perspective, a headlong dash down a kaleidoscope, yes. Stable light, daylight that didn't shift insanely through irritation into maddening thirst and back to animosity. Solid ground with regular up and down, salvation, Earth! He flung towards it and realized in mid-career: *No!*
Caught at the interface, he bounded on it, like a fly col-

lided with the web-thread of a spider, and in the moment of rebound saw; pale gray rocks crowned with brownish vegetation, overhead a slate-colored sky. Near the horizon a sun sinking, lurid red and not from sunset clouds. An old sun, chill and unfriendly.

He cried out and reversed, and was lost before the infinite choice of ways open to him. How do you invert a taste, a color and a not-quite square?

But . . .

"Jimmy! Jimmy, come back!"

His cry. Worked. But answered from . . . ? Tears streamed down his cheeks, little boy lost in the city, where's a friend to help me home? Beware of strangers who do dreadful things to little boys, always wait for the green before you cross, look out for funny cigarettes and funny pills . . .

Wait. Wait. Think. Be calm. Once, long ago, in a visited city: recollection of a sign which was not the right one, only identical, and then discovery of a threatening street, and . . . Oh, yes. He had remembered west by the sun. Used it, returned safe when artificial clues like names and neons failed. Parents worried since he was only nine—and he was seven, *seven,* and it was Mike who was nine and . . .

"Hey, Jimmy! *Jim-m-m-y!*"

Blindly, yet with assurance, he set off in the wake of that shrieking acid signal and prepared for the shock of yesterday which lay ahead. If felt as though he had to shred a million years.

But in the end there was a—form? Shape? Figure? It took hold of him, and wrenched him diagonally across eons, and somewhere on the way he lost himself.

Stop.

"Jim! Jim!"

Bending over him, person. Fair hair, anxious voice.

Greta. Others nearby: Mike, Porpentine, Natasha, Rick. He felt grass tickling, smelt air tinged with smoke. His throat was sore from half-remembered screaming.

Seeing him stir, Porpentine knelt, briskly touched his forehead, examined his eyes with a brush of his thumb to each upper lid, counted a dozen beats of his pulse. "Are you O.K.?" he demanded.

"I . . . Yes, I guess so," Waldron whispered. "Except I feel as though I've been through a mincing-machine. Someone help me sit up. And I'd like a drink of water."

"You're all right!" Greta exclaimed, clasping her hands. "Mike came out carrying you! We thought at first you were dead, and then—" She let the words die unspoken as the others gathered around, looking as though she could have bitten her tongue.

"You thought I'd gone weirdo," Waldron suggested, suddenly racked by shivers.

"Well—"

"Of course you did. Thanks"—to Rick, who had offered a canteen. He took three measured mouthfuls, savoring the stability of the clear taste which was not going to dissolve without warning into a blare of trumpets or the agony of amputation. And continued: "I guess it was a close call. In fact for a while I think I did go kind of crazy. Mike!"

Face concerned, Congreve bent towards him.

"Mike, I—I didn't mean to put a scare into you. But when the alien turned up—"

"What? What alien?"

"You mean you didn't see it? No, that's wrong. Hear it. A crashing noise. A tremendous crashing noise. I must have panicked."

"I don't get you," Congreve said after a pause. "When we got to that sort of a waterfall place—you know, the one we came to after the hundred steps—you seemed to become . . . I don't know! What would you call it? Petrified? As though you were mesmerized. I shouted at you, and you didn't react, and in the end I just had to drag you back."

"Petrified?" Waldron repeated incredulously. "But I ran off! I thought I'd never find my way back. And I wasn't in any waterfall place, as you call it."

Congreve hesitated. Glancing at Porpentine, he said, "Doc, I guess we'd better go home. It's going to take a long while to get to the bottom of all this."

"But I did run off!" Waldron insisted. "And what's more—" He licked his lips, while the others waited intently.

"What's more," he said at length. "I found my way to somewhere else. Bennett was right. I didn't go out, but I saw it. I saw a planet of another sun."

XXVII

"It works," Potter said a week later, and looked around the table, marveling at the optimism he could read on all these tired faces. Never, since the day the aliens struck, had he seen so many cheerful expressions in the same room.

Radcliffe said, "You mean Jim found his way back to the same place he stumbled on before."

"And this time I brought pictures to prove it," Waldron said, fanning a group of Polaroids that showed slate-blue sky, red sun, gray rocks, brown plants. "Thanks to Abramovitch. Without his analysis of the external color-signals I wouldn't have known when and where to go in. It looks as though you can enter the alien city anywhere, but the internal relationships are constantly changing. Alien city —oh, damn! I keep trying to use a better name, but the habit's so ingrained . . . Never mind. What counts is that we can apparently respond to the conditions inside. We can learn to recognize what are presumably the counterparts of direction-markings, the way a rat might cross a river on a fallen tree."

"But when you went in the first time," Radcliffe said, "how was it that you thought you ran off and Mike believed you were right next to him, and he thought you were in a place with a waterfall and you remembered something different, and . . . ? Come on, I want an explanation I can understand. I'm sick of merely being *told*."

Everyone looked at Porpentine, who shrugged and leaned back.

"You're asking a lot. After all, we've barely begun to study the problem. But it looks as though Jim's analogy will hold. A dog in a city can learn to cross the street only when the traffic's halted for a red light, without having to understand electricity. Pavel is still analyzing the readings he got from the instruments Jim took on his second trip, but one or two things have become clear, so I'll do my best to sum up what we know. Natasha, correct me if I say anything completely wrong, won't you?

"Both Mike and Jim agree that when they walked up to the wall they realized it was permeable and all they had to do was keep straight on. It is not in fact a wall, and we might have learned that long ago if we'd thought of using absolutely nonhostile means to test it, like touching it with a long pole. In fact, of course, what we've tried to touch it with have been rockets, bullets and laser beams, and anyone who was fool enough to push high energies at it was immediately driven insane."

"So if it's not a wall, what is it?" Radcliffe said.

"Something we have no words for. For the time being we've decided to call it an extraface—by analogy with interface. Under hypnosis Mike and Jim have both clearly described the sensations they felt when they reached it. Jim says it was like falling to arm's length from a tree-branch, Mike that it was like being spun around in a fast river-current. Pavel says there must be a local condition analogous to the boundary layer of a liquid, maybe even a macro equivalent of the surface tension on a nucleon; at any rate it seems to mark a change in the nature of space itself. During the transit, there's no idea of direction and the senses are hopelessly cross-connected, although will-power remains and the confusion is quite enjoyable. Mike said it was like a good drunk, and Jim—who incidentally had far more vivid sensory experiences—said it was like delirium but without the pain or sickness.

"As to what's inside . . . or outside, as they both insist on calling it: well, it is a *place*. In other words you get your sense of location back. But as well as that you acquire an awareness of 'uncountable directions, all lying ahead of you. They're agreed on this much, even though they differ on almost everything else. But it ties into a suggestion Orlando put forward, as I recall."

"Which one?" Potter said dryly. "I've had lots of ideas, and most of them have turned out to be wrong."

"You proposed that the aliens might think in a matrix mode, didn't you? And you also said they might omit verbalization when communicating data."

Potter nodded.

"Well, we're tentatively regarding this in terms of a multiplex data situation, but not quite the way you originally phrased it; more, we're comparing it to a modern city as a Bushman might see it, confused by the plethora of information making claims on your attention—advertisements, radio noise, TV, warnings, street-corner speakers and the rest. Only that's a terrible oversimplification. It does look as though beyond the extraface many, many different layers—volumes—segments—whatever you call them—many different bits of space-time, anyway, coexist, and can be perceived as simultaneous."

"But not to the same degree by everybody," Congreve put in. "Once we were through the extraface, so far as I was concerned it was possible, though hellish hard, to walk a hundred paces as arranged, stop and look around, come back to the point of entry . . . I interpreted my surroundings in rather conventional terms; Jim didn't. He must be far more sensitive to these space-time strata. Right, Louis?"

"I suspect so," Porpentine agreed. "You were convinced he never left your side on that first visit. He's absolutely certain he lost touch with you when a passing alien scared him and he fled down a direction which luckily he perceived as being labeled by—ah—some very peculiar coordinates."

Waldron chuckled. "Coordinates! Yes! I remember I was thinking about putting on well-matched clothes. Literally. I guess I must have been seven when I first learned that use of the word, and of course that was the age I'd been regressed to. Except—" He hesitated.

"Yes, *except,*" Porpentine said. "That brings us to an absolutely crucial point. You were right to suggest we might sneak past the aliens' defenses by using hypnosis. But for completely the wrong reasons."

Radcliffe started. "How's that again?"

"Regressing someone to an earlier age is of course a fiction. You don't wipe out the later memories. You can't. At most you can discount them. Fortunately for us, that's quite enough, combined of course with a good deal of conditioning, orders not to hate the aliens, not to touch or interfere with anything, and so on. The point is, though, that from the regressed age you can *remember in both directions.* Jim gave some vivid examples of this. He compared some of his sensations to the tingle of excitement which went with his awakening adolescent interest in girls' bodies, yet at seven he was still prepubescent, and is consciously aware that his sexual urge was dormant until he was twelve, while he didn't lose his virginity until he was seventeen. All these numbers got mixed up with his attempts to count a hundred paces, as well as his concern for his theoretical mental age. And when he was struggling to find his way back from the distant exit he chanced across, he says he clearly recalls preparing himself for the shock of yesterday, but he had to wait a hell of a long time before it arrived."

"Bennett," Radcliffe said. "He got turned around. Why didn't Mike and Jim?"

Porpentine spread his hands. "Pavel is working on the assumption that whatever the device was which he restored to working order, it must have lacked some associated mechanism, or field, which beyond the extraface prevents that kind of mishap. Compare it to having an accelerator and no brakes, or no steering. If you have to compare it to something, and I keep finding that I do."

"So it may be confusion of the time-sense which drives at least some weirdos out of their minds," Potter said.

"Yes, it may. But we're going to have to get rid of the blanket category 'weirdo'," Porpentine asserted. "When we study them in more detail, we'll almost certainly find there are a number of different types, some affected by the defensive field, some by time-confusion, some by the cross-connection of sensory data—like someone who can't come down again after an overdose of LSD—and some quite possibly by the shock of encountering an alien inside the—" He glanced ruefully at Waldron. "I was going to say 'city', too. I mean inside the transit nexus."

"That," Waldron muttered, "is a very alarming experience. Believe you me. We'll have to work out some means of detecting their approach. Not that the chance of meeting one of them seems to be very high."

There was a pause. Radcliffe said eventually, "The main point is, though, that with proper preparation we humans can learn the—the coordinates of the system, even if we don't have the least idea how they work. And sneak quietly through to other worlds."

"Yes, that's what we're hoping. We can't do it on the adult level, that's definite. Regression is going to remain essential, at least for the foreseeable future. The learning process is nonintellectual, like learning to swim, or ride a bicycle, or walk a tight-rope—in Jim's phrase, like learning to wiggle your ears. And it's notorious that it's best to start young when it comes to developing any talent that can't be verbalized. Music is the prime example."

"I get you," Radcliffe said. "When I was a kid I used to think music was kind of sissy. When I was about fifteen I got interested in guitar, but I never got to be any good. It was already too late."

"Pavel seems to have been right to suggest that in fact the aliens may not be very different from ourselves after all," Potter said. "At any rate we do seem to have the necessary mental equipment to make some sort of sense out of their processes. The necessary muscles, as it were—I'm thinking of Jim's ear-wiggling image. Given the proper incentive, even though we don't ordinarily have any use for them we can bring them under conscious control."

Porpentine nodded. "The next step I plan to take is an investigation of yoga techniques, to see if the kind of acquired skills which can reduce oxygen requirements or alter EEG waves offer any clues to what happens inside your mind when you cross the extraface. It's going to be a long project, this, but I'm confident of eventual success."

"Given some backing," Potter said. "Given personnel and funds. Den, could you have those Polaroids of Jim's copied, and extra prints made of all the film we've shot? I'm going to Washington, to scream and yell and raise Cain until those purblind idiots realize what's happened. I'm going to recruit physicists, engineers, astronomers, doctors, psychologists . . . I'm going to bring you more rats than you can handle."

"I get on best with my own kind," Radcliffe said.

Chuckling, Potter continued, "But before they arrive . . .

Mike, you'd better add a few trimmings to your scheme for taming the relidges."

"Mine?" Congreve said, laying a hand on his chest. "Well, I guess by adoption. Such as what?"

"Don't stop at half-measures. Don't simply imitate Brother Mark. Go the whole hog and call yourself the Archangel Michael, and preach on the text you mentioned yourself—'except ye become as little children'—and promise that you'll actually escort people into the holy city. We'll make arrangements to screen all the disciples you acquire, sort out those who are most susceptible to hypnosis, or drugs or yoga techniques according to what Louis's researches turn up, and then we'll hold private tuition for them in secret. I don't believe the nexi give access to only one other planet. I suspect it's more like thousands. After all, they've put five nexi on this planet alone, and so far as we can tell Earth is no more than an interchange station. By trial and error we should find the way to hundreds of different worlds."

"But they may not be fit for human life," Natasha said. "Suppose we send people through, and they die?"

"How many people died trying to repel Buishenko's invasion?" countered Potter. "How many are dying right now as the Chinese take over his territory? How many were casually blotted out by the aliens when they set off our nukes? Maybe we'll have to accept that some of the people who go out will become casualties, the way we do in wartime. They'll include some of our finest individuals, but hasn't war always taken the best instead of the worst? Surely it's better to risk death in the cause of all mankind than for the sake of some stupid political squabble that's going to be forgotten in a hundred years."

"Rats get on ships," Radcliffe said, as though the whole argument could be dismissed in those four words.

"Yes, but whatever you say, Den, we *aren't* rats. We're

human beings, with some guts, some intelligence, some capacity for planning ahead. And there's going to come a time when the aliens will wish they'd treated us with more respect!"

XXVIII

It would snow tonight for sure; the leaden overcast was threatening and the wind bore a keen edge. But Fred Johnson paid little attention to the state of the weather, like all the others standing patiently with him on the bleak hillside. His main reaction to the prospect of snow was vague regret that he would not see how glorious the heavenly city appeared when there was a mantle of white over the surrounding country.

By then, though, he would be *in* glory. . . .

He was an electronics engineer in ordinary life. Right now, however, he was first and foremost a disciple of the Archangel Michael. He had attended a relidge meeting out of sheer curiosity; afterwards he had been invited to talk privately with one of the apostles, and had agreed because he wanted to argue the guy out of his ridiculous convictions, and the tables had been completely turned on him. He had reached the unexpected conclusion, over prosaic coffee and doughnuts, that his greatest ambition was access to the angelic city. "Except ye become as little children . . . !" the archangel had thundered—and he had obeyed. He waited passive with the rest of today's Chosen, eyes fixed in adoration on the spectacular play of colors across the valley, and never for a moment wondered why he was hung about with tools and equipment: an axe, a shotgun and shells, a first-aid kit, a portable radio, a bag of food, seeds, extra clothing, a bedroll and a cookpot, a load he was just strong enough to carry at a fast walking pace.

All the others, too, carried similar burdens, including anything that might facilitate their survival—somewhere else. But he did not notice. He would not be able to until the post-hypnotic trigger buried in his subconscious during those sessions of "private tuition" in the mysteries of the angelic host were tripped by an external stimulus.

Then he would remember what the transit nexus really was.

A helicopter settled to the ground alongside the glass-fronted hut which overlooked the waiting group of Chosen. Radcliffe jumped out and walked—briskly, for the air was icy—towards its door.

The occupants nodded a greeting as he entered. Monitoring a screen on which was presented a continuous analysis of the color-patterns on the nexus—their instruments were linked by landline to Radcliffe's own computer, a very respectable three-and-a-half generation model—Pavel and Natasha were too busy to do more. Waldron and Greta were only checking equipment manifests, and could spare time to chat.

"Come to see them off?" Waldron inquired.

"Not exactly," Radcliffe said. "I brought some news from Orlando. Thought you might like to hear it before it turns up on the radio."

"Orlando?" Greta glanced up. "I thought he was still in Australia. Is he back?"

"No, this is a message from Canberra; Washington passed it on. They successfully infiltrated the city there at five A.M. our time and the reports look good."

"Another possible?" Waldron said eagerly.

"More than possible. They call it the best yet—a subtropical climate, green vegetation, no large animal life in the immediate vicinity . . . Of course, it'll be a long time before we can start shipping people to it, what with that bastard Villiers-Hart trying to grab back his ground, but it does sound kind of special, doesn't it?"

Waldron stared out of the window at the Chosen. It was a big group today, nearly eight hundred strong.

"You know, when I got that glimpse of Exit A on my first venture into the nexus, I was scared blind. I still don't know how I found my way home. And here we are in a matter of months equipped with route-finders small enough to drop in your pocket. I thought we'd abandoned hope, resigned from the business of thinking and decided to turn into vegetables. I can hardly believe so much has happened in such a short time."

"Speaking of route-finders," Greta said, reverting to her equipment lists, "you did hear, did you, that Pavel has confirmed his guess about Type Five artifacts? People are already starting to refer to them as compasses."

"I hadn't heard, but I'm not surprised. We thought of the aliens as being infinitely superior to us for far too long. We should have realized they had faults and shortcomings of their own as soon as we discovered they were capable of breaking things and throwing them away." Radcliffe moved to Waldron's side and pointed at the Chosen. "Where are they going, by the way?"

"This is the first follow-up party for Exit G," Waldron answered. "It's a trifle ahead of schedule, but today there's a good plain path—purple-salt-and-rubbery all the way. The advance guard has been there nine weeks, and they're very enthusiastic, and if we miss this route we may not get another good one for several months." He scanned a bank of clocks on the hut wall, which showed GMT, local time, sidereal time, corrected transit time—by which they scheduled the departure of the Chosen—and several new rhythms derived from observation of the cyclic color-changes on the extraface of the nexus. "Mike's late," he added. "He was due here two minutes ago. I hope nothing's gone wrong."

"I saw his 'copter on the way here," Radcliffe said. "Look, there it comes."

They glanced at the gray-shrouded sky. All the Chosen were doing the same. The arrival of "Archangel" Mike Congreve was the signal they were so anxiously awaiting. Up to the moment when he showed himself, doubts might linger about their chance of entering the heavenly city.

Doubting was over. A ragged cheer went up, and was followed by the chanting of a tune they had been taught as a reinforcement for their hypnotically imposed orders.

"Quite a guy, our Mike," Radcliffe said soberly.

True enough, Waldron signified with a nod. During the past few months his mind had been stocked with data concerning every route so far charted through the nexus. Even without a route-finder he could lead the Chosen through the swirling flows of color-as-taste, sound-as-pain and the rest, as easily as along a human street. So far he had guided parties totaling almost fourteen thousand to eight different habitable worlds.

Of course, "habitable" would remain a questionable description for generations. Some plague might spring up, some long-term effect of alien chemicals in what appeared to be safe soil or clean rain might depress intelligence, some parasite or predator might emerge from hibernation . . . But there was a slim chance, worth taking, of ultimate survival.

There had been casualties, as predicted: a few right here, people whose hypnotic armor failed them, who returned as weirdos, and others on the far side of exits now classified as dangerous, who had ventured through and never returned. Later, the better facilities and more

knowledge of what the aliens would and would not tolerate, someone would investigate their fate. Not yet. There
was too much else to be done.

"It's a hell of a big batch," Radcliffe muttered. "Isn't it
risky to send so many at once?"

"You think the aliens will be annoyed?" Greta said.

"It's a possibility."

"I guess you're right. But since we quit pilfering live artifacts, the aliens have shown no sign of even noticing us. I
suspect they can't be bothered to. We've put up with rats
and mice for thousands of years, and we only take steps
against them when they cause direct harm: rob the larder,
carry plague."

"Yes, but suppose we affect them in some way we don't
know about," Radcliffe objected. "Mice stink, for example. That's regarded as a good reason to poison them."

"We'll go on taking that chance," Waldron grunted.
"I'd rather risk that than be in Asia, wouldn't you?"

Radcliffe shuddered visibly. "Damned right. The way it
started off, I thought the Chinese would just roll Buishenko
up tidily and put him away, and the world would be a lot
quieter. Then of course the loyalist Russian forces intervened . . . How many casualties so far? Twenty million, is
it?"

"Can we have silence, please?" Natasha called, and
picking up a microphone went on without a pause. "Mike,
the colors are coming up to Exit G pattern now, and they
should take about two minutes fifteen seconds to stabilize.
When you get three green ripples moving right to left,
you'll have six minutes forty seconds to complete your
pep-talk, and you get moving on a recurrent flash of rust
and gold."

"Fine!" came the whispered reply. Congreve had a contact mike taped to his throat for messages he didn't want
the Chosen to overhear. As for his earphones, they were

concealed by a static-aura halo of a handsome electric blue which Abramovitch, laughing like a hyena, had personally designed and built for him. It went splendidly with his luminescent robe of white and silver.

And, a moment later, he started to deliver his final address in a monstrously amplified voice that made the ill-carpentered window of the hut rattle in its frame.

His job for the moment over, Abramovitch leaned back and gave a mountainous sigh. He said something to Natasha which made her laugh, and she translated. In the past months he had learned some English, but he was still far from fluent.

"Pavel says he is like a man in a post office, or the ticket clerk at an airport, yes? Always hearing about distant places and never seeing any himself because he gets too little pay for foreign vacations. Now doubtless they will ask him to go to Australia, and he will have been all around this planet and still not have traveled properly."

"He's right," Waldron said. "In fact he's so damned right I think it's painful. I'm going to quit my job. I'm not very good at it, you know."

Radcliffe glanced at him in surprise. "But you've made nearly as many transits as Mike, haven't you?"

"Sure, sure. I've been through Exit G and seen a bird as big as an eagle which wasn't a bird but the detachable crown of a tree. I've been through Exit K and seen a rock that wasn't a rock but a colony of creatures as hard as marble. I've been lots of places. But I'm too sensitive. I cross-refer sense-data too readily. Louis has to give me tranquilizers now—and did you know I came back from one trip with a burn on my arm because somebody shouted too loud?"

"Is that a fact?" Radcliffe said incredulously.

"Oh, yes. I had a blister the size of my palm. It's healed O.K., but . . . No, I'm going to quit and join the Chosen."

"So am I," Greta said, putting aside her equipment lists. "I'm going to see Louis tomorrow, find out if I'm suitable for hypnosis. Not that that's so important anymore, with the new drugs they're using."

"I'll be damned," Radcliffe muttered. "Know something? You're turning out to be better rats than I am."

"You're not going anywhere?" Greta suggested.

"Me? No, the project's too long-term to appeal to me. The best we can hope for is to plant colonies and creep around under the aliens' feet. Sure, it's a great scheme, because it means if they ever get sick enough of us to sterilize Earth we can hope to leave descendants elsewhere. If that does happen, though . . . Well, look at the way we've messed up this planet, even though it is our own home. We damned well can't afford to make the same mistakes anywhere else, right? So it's best to let my type stay behind."

There was a brief silence. Then, as though embarrassed at having spoken so nakedly, he shrugged his coat tighter around him. "Must be going. Maura and the kid are waiting in the 'copter."

The door slammed behind him.

"Hasn't Den changed?" Waldron said in a low voice.

"We all have," Greta said. "We've *been* changed. It's a great thing to have hope again, even a slender hope like ours."

"Yes, but that's not all. Maybe it's not the most important." He frowned, struggling to find words. "I think of it more like this. We've been desperately trying to make the world seem familiar again. We've been using comparisons and analogies: Den with his rats and mice, Orlando with his peasants under an army of occupation, Louis with his Bushman in a modern city, and so on. Finally we've begun to admit that this isn't the same as anything we've run across before. It isn't even much *like* anything else. How could it be? We've been tossed without warning clear over the horizon of our own past. We calculated that the odds were against our being alone in the galaxy. Now we know we're not. We deduced that other stars must have planets. Now we can go and walk on them. It's a clean break. It's killed our past. We can't live in it or by its standards anymore. All that counts from now on and forever is the future."

He broke off, for the others weren't listening. They were staring with aching, longing eyes across the valley. One by one, following with perfect confidence in the steps of the archangel who led them, the Chosen were leaving for their appointment with destiny on a world for which there had not yet been time to coin a name.

When the last of them had dissolved into the incomprehensible web of forces which would shrink interstellar vastness to the dimensions of a morning stroll, Waldron glanced at Greta.

"Have you decided what exit you want to go through?"

"Yes."

"Mind if I pick the same one?"

"Good idea."

Smiling, he leaned back in his chair. And thought: *so rats get on ships . . . True. And what I'm going to do is much the same. But I'm not going to do it as a rat. I'm going to do it as a man.*

At long last the sky began to shed the first of its threatened flakes of snow.

11
NOVELS BY
ROBERT A. HEINLEIN

055004	Between Planets 95c
106005	Citizen of the Galaxy 95c
318006	Have Space Suit-Will Travel 95c
711408	Red Planet 95c
733303	Rocket Ship Galileo 95c
734400	The Rolling Stones 95c
777300	Space Cadet 95c
780007	The Star Beast 95c
811257	Time for the Stars 95c
826602	Tunnel in the Sky 95c
915025	The Worlds of Robert A. Heinlein 95c

Available wherever paperbacks are sold or use this coupon.

ace books, (Dept. MM) Box 576, Times Square Station
New York, N.Y. 10036

Please send me titles checked above.

I enclose $................Add 15¢ handling fee per copy.

Name ....

Address ....

City..................... State............. Zip........

Please allow 4 weeks for delivery.   17B

EDGAR RICE
BURROUGHS

Just 75c Each

092023	Carson of Venus
092825	Cave Girl
215624	Escape on Venus
470211	Land Time Forgot
492926	The Lost Continent
495028	Lost on Venus
537027	Moon Maid
537522	Moon Men
644823	Out of Time's Abyss
665026	The Pirates of Venus
798520	Tarzan at the Earth's Core

Available wherever paperbacks are sold or use this coupon.

A. E. Van Vogt

048603	The Battle of Forever	95c
104109	Children of Tomorrow	95c
137984	Darkness on Diamondia	95c
228114	The Far Out Worlds of A. E. Van Vogt	75c
697003	Quest For the Future	95c
765008	The Silkie	60c
871814	The War Against the Rulls	$1.25
878553	The Weapon Shops of Isher	60c

JOHN BRUNNER

033001	The Atlantic Abomination	60c
166686	Dramaturges of Yan	75c
381210	Jagged Orbit	$1.25
524009	Meeting at Infinity	60c
812701	Times Without Number	60c
822106	Traveler in Black	75c

Available wherever paperbacks are sold or use this coupon.

WINNER OF
THE HUGO AWARD
AND THE
NEBULA AWARD
FOR BEST
SCIENCE FICTION
NOVEL OF
THE YEAR

045922 **Babel 17** Delaney   95c

062190 **Big Time** Leiber   95c

106229 **City** Simak   95c

166413 **Dragon Masters** Vance
The Last Castle Vance   95c

167023 **Dream Master** Zelazny   95c

172619 **Dune** Herbert $1.25

196824 **Einstein Intersection** Delany   95c

249011 **Four for Tomorrow** Zelazny   95c

478008 **Left Hand of Darkness** LeGuin   95c

727826 **Rite of Passage** Panshin   95c

806927 **This Immortal** Zelazny   95c

Available wherever paperbacks are sold or use this coupon.